*"I don't think you realize the trouble
you could get yourself into. With
me...or any man,"*

Charlie whispered.

Any man could never make her feel like this,
Violet knew. Just the idea of feeling his lips
against hers made her head reel. But as for trouble,
she'd grown up with it, lived with it, and was still
trying to get out of it.

"Trouble is my middle name, Ranger Pardee.
But it isn't your problem," Violet said, hating the
sound of her breathy voice and the thrill she was
feeling at being so close to him.

She was right. It *wasn't* his problem. And he knew
he should load her up right now, this very minute,
and haul her into town. But he also knew he
couldn't.

"I'm a Texas Ranger. My job is dealing with trouble,
before or after it happens. And—" suddenly he had
her in his arms again "—it looks like right now, my
job is you."

D0048713

Dear Reader,

August is jam-packed with exciting promotions and top-notch authors in Silhouette Romance! Leading off the month is RITA Award-winning author Marie Ferrarella with *Suddenly...Marriage!*, a lighthearted VIRGIN BRIDES story set in sultry New Orleans. A man and woman, both determined to remain single, exchange vows in a mock ceremony during Mardi Gras, only to learn their bogus marriage is for real....

With over five million books in print, Valerie Parv returns to the Romance lineup with *Baby Wishes and Bachelor Kisses*. In this delightful BUNDLES OF JOY tale, a confirmed bachelor winds up sole guardian of his orphaned niece and must rely on the baby-charming heroine for daddy lessons—*and* lessons in love. Stella Bagwell continues her wildly successful TWINS ON THE DOORSTEP series with *The Ranger and the Widow Woman*. When a Texas Ranger discovers a stranded mother and son, he welcomes them into his home. But the pretty widow harbors secrets this lawman-in-love needs to uncover.

Carla Cassidy kicks off our second MEN! promotion with *Will You Give My Mommy a Baby?* A 911 call from a five-year-old boy lands a single mom and a true-blue, red-blooded hero in a sticky situation that quickly sets off sparks. *USA Today* bestselling author Sharon De Vita concludes her LULLABIES AND LOVE miniseries with *Baby and the Officer*. A crazy-about-kids cop discovers he's a dad, but when he goes head-to-head with his son's beautiful adoptive mother, he realizes he's fallen head over heels. And Martha Shields rounds out the month with *And Cowboy Makes Three*, the second title in her COWBOYS TO THE RESCUE series. A woman who wants a baby and a cowboy who needs an heir agree to marry but discover the honeymoon is just the beginning....

Don't miss these exciting stories by Romance's unforgettable storytellers!

Enjoy,

Joan Marlow Golan

Joan Marlow Golan
Senior Editor Silhouette Books

Please address questions and book requests to:
Silhouette Reader Service
U.S.: 3010 Walden Ave., P.O. Box 1325, Buffalo, NY 14269
Canadian: P.O. Box 609, Fort Erie, Ont. L2A 5X3

STELLA Baswell

THE RANGER AND THE WIDOW WOMAN

Silhouette

R O M A N C E™

Published by Silhouette Books

America's Publisher of Contemporary Romance

SILHOUETTE BOOKS

ISBN 0-373-19314-9

THE RANGER AND THE WIDOW WOMAN

Copyright © 1998 by Stella Bagwell

This edition published by arrangement with Harlequin Books S.A.

Printed in U.S.A.

Books by Stella Bagwell

STELLA BAGWELL

sold her first book to Silhouette in November 1985. Now, more than thirty novels later, she is still thrilled to see her books in print and can't imagine having any other job than that of writing about two people falling in love.

She lives in a small town in southeastern Oklahoma with her husband of twenty-six years. She has one son and daughter-in-law.

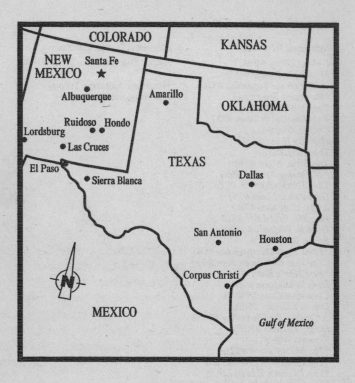

Chapter One

Charlie Pardee was hot, tired and hungry. The last thing he wanted to do was stop on the side of a blistering highway and play mechanic. The temperature was ninety-five degrees in the shade, if a shade could be found within a twenty-mile radius. But the lady standing helplessly by the fender of the dark blue sedan had the prettiest legs he'd seen in a long time, and Charlie was not a man who could ignore a lady in distress, even though every part of his brain was begging him to.

He parked on the opposite shoulder from the ailing car. Once he was on the ground and out of his pickup truck, he lifted his straw cowboy hat and swiped long fingers through the sandy brown hair plastered to his damp forehead. It wasn't a day for anyone, man or woman, to be stranded in a New Mexican desert.

Plopping the bent straw back on his head, he sauntered across the lonely highway. "Having trouble, ma'am?"

The woman's dark eyes studied Charlie's tall, muscular form as if she couldn't quite decide whether he was an angel sent to save her or a demon she should be running from.

"I...uh...think my car is overheated."

Steam was billowing out from under the hood, and she had to think on the matter. He'd come up on a real nitwit this time, Charlie decided.

"It surely appears that way," he said drily.

He moved closer to the woman and the small sedan. Her wary gaze not daring to leave him, she inched backwards, her hand fumbling for the door handle.

Charlie couldn't imagine how she thought getting back into a broken down car was going to save her from his clutches. But at least she had enough common sense to be on her guard. That was more than he could say for most women.

He gestured toward the car. "If you'll pop the hood, I'll take a look. I'm not a mechanic, but I might be able to tell you what's wrong. Have you been having trouble with the car before?"

She shook her head, then seeming to decide she had no choice but to trust him, she opened the car door and leaned in to pull the latch.

With the hood released, Charlie pushed it up the rest of the way and propped it there. The woman, who couldn't have been more than twenty-four or -five, appeared at the front of the car to stand a few steps away from him.

From the corner of his eye, Charlie caught another glimpse of her bare, slender legs. She was wearing navy blue boxer shorts and a lime green T-shirt. Leather thongs were on her feet. Her pale, smooth skin told him she wasn't a sun worshiper. The pearly pink color of her toenails assured him she was proud of her femininity, but she didn't like to flaunt it. She wasn't a glamor girl by any means, but she certainly had the makings for one.

"I haven't had any trouble with the car before now,"

she said in a soft drawl that was a bit Texan, but mostly Georgian. "All of a sudden a bell started dinging and a light on the dash said Check Engine. What does that mean?"

"It means you're in trouble," Charlie said flatly.

Her dark, winged brows shot upward as though she was certain she'd heard him wrong. "I beg your pardon?"

Charlie had seen a lot of pretty women in his twenty-nine years, and being the normal red-blooded male he was, he usually gave them a look whenever one passed his way. This woman, however, was leaving him with the idiotic urge to stare.

"The car," he explained with an annoyed frown, then forced his eyes to the steaming engine. "'Check Engine' means it's a pretty sick puppy."

"Oh." A heavy sigh passed her pink lips. "I certainly hope that isn't the case. I'm not prepared to have major repairs done to the car."

Quickly identifying the problem, Charlie picked up a piece of broken fan belt and held it up for her to view. "The belt that runs the cooling system has broken. If you're lucky, and the engine didn't get too hot, it will only be a minor repair job."

Raking her tumbled hair off her face, she glanced up at the tall man with eyes as blue as the sky overhead. "How close is the nearest town to the west?"

It never ceased to amaze him how people would start across desolate land without so much as a road map, but he resisted the urge to lecture her. "About twenty-five miles or more."

His hand resting on the hood, Charlie covertly studied her. She was a little thing, the top of her head barely reaching the middle of his upper arm. Her hair was a dark cloud of waves around her head and shoulders. Her ivory complexion was satin smooth and gleamed with perspiration.

But it was her pale green eyes that struck him the most. The color of a tropic sea, they were incredibly beautiful. Yet they were also full of secrets and suspicions.

Ten years of being a lawman allowed Charlie to see things a normal person would never notice. And he couldn't help wondering what had brought this woman out to the desert.

"Twenty-five miles," she repeated uncertainly. "If the car could—"

"Mommy? Mommy?"

Thinking she'd been traveling alone, Charlie was surprised to see a young boy around four or five hanging his head out the back window of the vehicle. His short, curly hair was dark like his mother's, but the resemblance stopped there.

The woman quickly moved to her son. "It's all right, Sam," she gently assured him. "I'm right here."

The child scrubbed the last crumbs of sleep from his eyes, then, leaning further out the window, he glanced curiously around him. "What's the matter, Mommy? Why are we stopped?"

She smoothed her hand alongside his cheek. "Something is wrong with the car, honey. We have to wait a little while before we can go again."

"Uh…ma'am," Charlie felt compelled to interrupt. "No 'little while' will fix anything. You can't drive this car two feet until a mechanic puts a new belt on it. He might be able to do the job here. But I'm betting it will have to be towed to the nearest garage."

Charlie watched her press small fingers against both temples. There was no wedding ring on her left hand or even a pale band where one had been in the past. A single mother. A divorcee or widow. She could be any of the three, he decided.

"I see. What you're telling me is that my son and I are well and truly stranded."

"You were...until I got here."

She didn't know what that was supposed to mean and she wasn't about to ask. "Then what do you propose I do?"

Charlie had been on his way home to his parents' ranch north of Hondo. But what the hell, he figured, he'd been forced to put his homecoming off several times in the past six months. An hour or two more wouldn't kill him. Besides, he couldn't leave her and the kid here to the mercy of the searing heat and whatever nut case might happen to be driving by. "You can ride in with me. Or I have a cellular phone in my truck you can use to call for a wrecker service to come get you."

Leaving her car and climbing into a vehicle with a stranger was not a choice Violet O'Dell wanted to make. Even if the stranger was the sexiest thing she'd seen in a long time.

"I'd really rather not leave my car," she told him. "I'll be glad to pay you for the use of your telephone. But I don't have the slightest idea who to call."

Charlie had been away from the area too long to know a reliable mechanic to call, but he knew someone who would. "I'll get somebody out here."

He crossed the highway to his white truck and opened the door on the shoulder side. To his surprise, the woman ordered her son to stay in the car, then walked across the highway to join him.

Glancing at her strained features, Charlie punched in a number, then put the telephone to his ear.

While he waited for the connection to go through, she asked, "Are you from around these parts?"

"My parents live on a ranch about thirty miles from here." The dispatcher on the other end of the line answered, and Charlie turned his attention away from the woman. "Yes," he spoke into the mouthpiece. "Is Sheriff Pardee in? This is his son, Charlie."

The woman gasped softly, and her eyes widened as she stared at him. "Sheriff? I don't need—what are you doing?" she suddenly demanded. "I haven't done anything wrong!"

Frowning, he shook his head at her just as the dispatcher informed him the sheriff was out of the office at the moment. "Can Randall come to the phone?" he asked the woman.

As he waited to speak to the undersheriff, he said to Violet, "I didn't say you had done anything wrong, Miss— uh, did you tell me your name?"

Her lips pursed with disapproval, she glanced at him sharply. "I didn't. But it's Violet—O'Dell."

He thrust his hand toward her. "Hello, Violet. I'm Charles Pardee. Call me Charlie. Everyone else does."

She didn't want to touch him. Not that there was one repulsive thing about the man. On the contrary, he was the most appealing male she'd encountered in a long time. His slightly square jaws, strong, dented chin and striking blue eyes made his looks more than nice. But for some inexplicable reason she was scared to touch him, afraid she might feel a sizzle of attraction for this stranger.

"Hey, Randall," he suddenly spoke into the phone. "How's it going? This is Charlie."

With his hand still offered to hers, Violet had little choice but to put her palm alongside his. His long, lean fingers quickly enveloped hers, and she swallowed hard as warmth filled her cheeks.

To Violet's relief, however, he seemed to consider the encounter as nothing more than a brief handshake. As soon as he dropped his hold on her, he turned his full attention to the person on the other end of the line.

"Yeah, I'm back home for a little vacation. They got sick of looking at me back in Forth Worth. Is my dad around? No, it's nothing about a case. I'm out here on Highway 380 about twenty-five miles east of Picacho. There's a lady here with a broken fan belt. I didn't know who would be the best mechanic to call. Can you send one with a tow truck out here?"

He looked over at Violet, then grunted with sardonic amusement. Violet's spine stiffened.

"Okay, bud, I'll warn her. And thanks, Randall."

"Warn me?"

"Randall says you ought to know I can't be trusted."

The expression on his face held little humor, if any. Yet surely he had to be teasing. It was difficult to tell what this stranger was all about.

"Who was that you were speaking to?" she asked him.

"The undersheriff of this county," he said matter-of-factly. "He works for my dad, Roy Pardee, the Sheriff."

She stared at him with something akin to horror. "Look, Mr....uh, Charlie Pardee. I don't want the law out here! I want someone to fix my car!"

She was getting more agitated with each passing second and Charlie's weariness changed to skepticism. "You have something against the law?"

Scarlet color splashed across her cheeks. "No. Why? Are you going to tell me you're some sort of lawman, too?" she asked incredulously.

For an answer he pulled a square of leather from his jeans pocket then flopped it open for her inspection. Violet stepped closer, and her face paled considerably as she read the name inscribed on the badge. Charles Pardee, Texas Ranger.

Dear Lord, how had she managed to run smack into a lawman? A *Texas* lawman at that! Now just calm down, Violet, she silently scolded herself. No one knows you're gone yet. And this man just happened to be going down the same road. That was all there was to this whole thing.

"What…are you doing out here?" she asked, trying to sound as casual as possible.

Her eyes scanned his faded jeans and cowboy boots, the plain white T-shirt covering his broad shoulders. Didn't Texas Rangers wear a badge on their chest and a gun belt on their hips? This guy looked as though he'd just stepped out of a cattle pen.

Charlie didn't know why he was taking the time to explain anything to this woman. He was hot enough to melt. He wanted to go home, put up his feet, drink a cold beer and try to forget the past year of his life. "We Rangers do stray out of the state from time to time," he said sardonically.

She nervously fingered the tiny heart-shaped locket dangling against the hollow of her throat. "Then I guess I should be thankful you happened to stray this way. This highway doesn't appear to be heavily traveled."

"The traffic usually depends on what's going on in Ruidoso. A big futurity at the Downs or a festival of some sort always brings a string of traffic to this highway." His blue eyes continued to rake a shrewd path over her face. "You headed very far?"

She hesitated, then nodded. "I'm just passing through New Mexico."

"Mommy! Can I get out of the car now?"

"Excuse me," she told Charlie, then crossed the highway to her son.

Through the open windows of his pickup cab, Charlie watched her open the back door of the sedan and lift her son out to the ground. He was dressed in shorts and sandals and a muscle shirt with some sort of action hero printed on the front. For a dark-headed child at this time of summer, he was pale. Charlie wondered if the little guy was sickly or if Violet O'Dell was overprotective and kept her son housed up most of the time. Either way, he hated the idea of a youngster, especially a boy, not being able to enjoy the outdoors.

Charlie put the cellular phone back in its cradle, then after a moment of thoughtful hesitation, walked across the highway to join the two of them.

The child tilted his head back and looked up at him with curious brown eyes. "My name is Sam," he said with a small measure of shyness. "What's yours?"

Charlie couldn't remember the last time he'd been around a child. Except for his cousin Emily's new baby, who had been born about four months ago, the rest of his family was grown-up. A few of his fellow Rangers had children, but he rarely saw any of them. And the juveniles he sometimes came in contact with through his work couldn't be compared to this innocent little fella.

Not certain how to greet a youngster of this age, he decided a handshake would have to do. "My name is Charlie. Nice to meet you, Sam."

"It's too hot in the car," he explained. "Mommy says she can't turn on the air conditioner."

The boy had a round face, dimples and a sprinkling of faint freckles across the bridge of his nose. As Charlie looked at the child, the detective instincts in him were wondering where his father was and why he and his mother were out here driving across the desert alone.

"Your mommy told you right," he told the boy. "She can't turn on the air conditioner now. Maybe you'd like to go sit in that bit of shade right over there."

Charlie pointed to a single twisted limb of juniper about fifteen feet away from the car. Other than a few clumps of sage and a yucca plant now and then, the sole evergreen was the only thing big enough to cast any sort of shade from the burning sun.

Violet shot Charlie a wary glance. "Do you think it would be safe? What about sidewinders or scorpions?"

It was all Charlie could do not to roll his eyes and curse out loud. As a child, the desert had been his playground. His mother had protected him and taught him about the dangers to watch for, but she hadn't smothered him. Like Charlie, Justine Pardee had been raised in this high desert country. She felt at home in it, whereas Violet O'Dell obviously didn't.

Biting his tongue, Charlie reminded himself he'd be home soon and this little delay would be nothing more than a dim, unpleasant memory. "Sidewinders or scorpions could be anywhere out here. Even in your bed. A person just has to be mindful of them."

Her mouth popped open with shocked disgust. "Not in my bed!"

Charlie's eyes cut a path over her slender figure. As far as he was concerned having Violet O'Dell in his bed would be far more dangerous than bugs or reptiles. She was the kind of woman that would get inside a man's head and be hell to get out.

"Look ma'am—er, Violet, the risk of your son getting a serious sunburn is far greater than him getting a snake- or bug-bite."

Violet had to concede he was probably right, but that didn't mean she wanted her son traipsing over unknown ground. And she certainly didn't want a man telling her what she ought or ought not do. Especially a man who made it sound as though her ignorance of the desert was grating on his nerves. She hadn't flagged the man down and begged for his help!

Not bothering to wait for her permission, Charlie reached for the child's hand. "Come on, Sam. I'll take you over to the shade. It's going to be a while before the man gets here to fix the car."

The two of them reached the juniper and Charlie examined the ground all around it, then called over to Violet, who was still standing beside the car watching them intently.

In a sardonic voice, he called out to her, "Nothing but dirt. So you can quit wringing your hands. It's too hot for even a horned toad to be out today."

Sam cocked his head up at Charlie. "What's a horned toad?" he asked curiously.

Charlie showed the child where to sit, then squatted down on his boot heels beside him. "Do you know what a lizard is?"

His dark eyes glued to Charlie's face, he nodded. "I've seen one before on the sidewalk. Mommy told me not to touch them."

No doubt, Charlie thought wryly. To Sam he said, "Well, a horned toad is a type of lizard, but he looks like a frog with horns."

"Oh! Is he dangerous?"

Dangerous? Good Lord, he felt like going over to Violet O'Dell right this minute and telling the woman she needed therapy or her son was going to grow up frightened of his own shadow. Or maybe the two of them simply needed a man in their life.

"Naw, there's nothing dangerous about him. When I was a boy like you I use to play with them all the time. I even kept one in a shoe box under my bed and fed him flies."

The expression on Sam's face said he didn't believe Charlie had ever been as little as himself. It also said the outdoors and all it held was an unknown fascination to him.

Back at the car Violet dug a few bills out of her purse, then carried them over to the Ranger. She didn't especially like the idea of being out here alone in the desert while waiting for a tow truck. But there wasn't any point in keeping the man here any longer. He'd already gone out of his way to help them. Moreover, Violet didn't want the lawman getting too friendly with Sam. Her son was usually talkative. She didn't want him inadvertently telling the man something about their life he didn't need to know.

"Here's something for the telephone call," she said, offering the bills to him. "If it's not enough, just say so."

A frown puckered Charlie's forehead as he glanced up at her. "I don't want your money."

She turned away from his probing blue eyes and back to her broken car. "Maybe you don't, but I prefer to pay you."

The cool, impersonal tone of her voice irked Charlie. He didn't deserve it. He'd already gone out of his way to help the woman. Besides, the frosty attitude didn't suit her at all.

His gaze lingered on the curve of her waist and the flare of her hips. "You don't like accepting help from strangers, is that it?"

Her back still to him she said, "I simply don't want to take advantage of your kindness, Ranger Pardee. You've already gone out of your way to help. Please don't feel as if you need to stay until the tow truck gets here. Sam and I will be fine now."

She was dismissing him, urging him to go. Charlie should be laughing with relief and hightailing it out of here as fast as he could go.

But for some reason, whether it was Sam's endearing little face or Violet O'Dell's lovely legs, he decided he couldn't simply walk away and leave them alone in the desert. He wouldn't be able to live with himself if he drove away and then heard later that something bad had happened to them.

"No, I think I'd better stay and make sure the tow truck gets here." To make his point, he sat down on the hot loamy soil beside her son. "If I were you," he added mat-

ter-of-factly to Violet, "I'd take a seat, too. This heat can
sap you before you know what's happening."

Carefully taking a seat on the opposite side of her son,
Violet gathered her knees to her chest. "Are you here in
New Mexico on business, Charlie?"

He propped his elbows on his bent knees. He didn't want
to think about *his business*. He was too tired, too weary of
it all. And this woman didn't really care. She was merely
making conversation. Other than his mother, he didn't
know any woman that really cared. "No, I'm on my way
home," he said flatly.

"Home? Isn't Texas your home?"

"Most of the time. But my parents' place, The Pardee
Ranch, is what I call my real home. It's where I always go
when I have a little vacation." Whenever he needed to get
away from the stress and strain of his job, when he needed
to get back under blue New Mexican skies, get the earth
back beneath his feet and remember why he'd ever become
a Ranger in the first place. And this time, he thought wearily, he needed the solitude more than he ever had in his
young life.

"Me and Mommy are on an adventure," Sam spoke up
brightly. "We're gonna see and do lots of new things."

Charlie glanced at the boy while his mind was turning
over all sorts of scenarios concerning Violet. Was she leaving a lover, a husband or simply a bad past? Hell, Charlie,
he chided himself, you need to quit questioning this
woman's motives. She was probably traveling to see rela-
tives or simply on a vacation, like he was supposed to be.
For the next few weeks he needed to quit being a Texas
Ranger and simply be a man.

"That sounds like fun," Charlie said in afterthought.

"It was fun until we became stranded," Violet remarked.
"The car isn't but three years old and I've taken very good
care of it. I never expected something like this to happen."

Once again Charlie had to stifle the urge to lecture the woman, to warn her to always be prepared for the unexpected. But it wasn't his place. Her husband or whoever had been the father of her child should have already done that. Besides, she would probably get the idea he was some sort of paranoid maniac. And maybe he was, he thought sourly.

"Heat like today's can cause things to happen to the best of cars."

A tractor trailer rig appeared on the eastern horizon. It whizzed by Violet's car and Charlie's truck without so much as a slack in speed, then less than five minutes later a car approached from the west. When it obviously slowed and started to pull onto the shoulder, Charlie stood up and waved it on.

"Mommy, I'm thirsty," Sam whined. "Are we gonna have to stay here much longer?"

"I don't know how much longer we'll be here, Sam. But sit where you are and I'll get some water from the car."

Violet left the pitiful excuse of a shade and headed to the car. Sam picked up a twig and made a long scratch in the dirt. "My mommy is nice."

Sam's words of adoration didn't surprise Charlie. At his age, he'd thought his own mother was wonderful. He still did. He loved and respected his father, and the two of them had always gotten on splendidly once his father had discovered he had a son. But when Charlie needed to spill his troubles, it was his mother he went to.

"She seems very nice," Charlie absently agreed as his thoughts drifted longingly to his quiet little cabin on the ranch. It had been months since he'd been away from ringing phones, faxes and pagers, city traffic, smog and the never-ending weight of a heavy workload. The solitude of the place would be like sheer heaven.

"She hasn't cried at all today," Sam spoke again. "And I'm glad."

The child's statement jerked Charlie out of his wishful thinking. From the corner of his eye, he watched the boy continue to dig a miniature trench in the sand. "Does your mother cry a lot?" he asked carefully.

Sam nodded, and Charlie was surprised at how much the child's grave expression touched him. For the past year he'd been numb. He'd thought he'd gone beyond feeling much of anything for anybody.

"Yeah," Sam answered. "Since my daddy went to heaven to live with the angels. Before then she only cried a little."

Charlie was at a loss for any sort of suitable reply, and when Violet returned with a bottle of flavored water, he figured it was just as well. Being a detective for the past three years, he knew how to get information from people. But he had no desire to pump this child. Sam had already told him enough to make him feel like an interloper, and he didn't want to care about these two. He really didn't want to care about anyone. It was too much work, too much pain.

Fifteen minutes later a wiry little man in greasy, striped overalls and no shirt arrived in a wrecker. Charlie assisted him as best he could while he replaced the broken belt, but when the mechanic tried to start the engine it refused.

"Just how hot was this car?" the little man directed at Violet.

She glanced helplessly at Charlie, then back to the mechanic. "All I know is a bell started dinging and steam poured out from beneath the hood."

The man shook his head and clucked his tongue. "Can't say right now, ma'am, but I'm afraid you've busted your heads."

"My heads?" she repeated blankly. "I'm sorry, but I

don't know anything about engines. Are you talking about something serious?''

"Sure enough. A two-day job at the least," he took off his greasy cap and thoughtfully scratched the top of his head. "And that's if the heads don't have to be shipped from a dealer in Albuquerque. But I'm bettin' they will. This is not your everyday make of car runnin' down the road."

Violet's heart sank as she watched the older man jab a cigarette between his lips and stick a lighter flame to the end. "This sounds like it could be expensive," she said.

He nodded grimly. "Might as well warn you, the heads alone, I'm figurin', will cost six or seven hundred. That's not countin' me takin' the cracked ones off and puttin' the new ones on."

"Oh, dear." Violet hadn't counted on anything like this happening. She was carrying a fairly large sum of cash with her, but not enough to pay for repairing the car. She had money in the bank back in Amarillo, but she'd planned on waiting as long as she could before she drew on it. She didn't want any sort of transactions showing up and tipping Rex off to her whereabouts.

"I suppose I'll have to let you tow the car into Ruidoso. But after that—I just don't have the money to pay for such major repairs. Is there some place I can store the car for a while?"

Up until now Charlie hadn't said anything. After all, she was a stranger. It wasn't any of his business what she did with her vehicle, herself or her child. And he was on vacation, damn it. The last thing he needed was to hassle himself with a woman and kid. But if she needed help or advice he could hardly refuse.

"Violet, if you have to be somewhere at a certain time, you could take the bus and come back and get your car later," he suggested.

Her green eyes swept up to his face, and in spite of his reluctance to get involved, Charlie felt himself crumbling like a piece of soft sandstone.

"There's no need for us to catch a bus. I don't…have a schedule to meet," she told him haltingly. "Like Sam told you…we just packed up and headed out on an adventure. I suppose—" She bit down on her lip while glancing back at the sick engine beneath the hood. "I'll have to find a job of some sort before I can afford to repair my car. Is there any sort of job for a woman in Ruidoso?"

Hellfire, she needed an employment agency, not him, Charlie wanted to yell at her. Instead, he took a deep breath and motioned for the mechanic to go ahead with the towing. Then, taking Violet by the upper arm, he led her to where Sam was still waiting patiently beneath the juniper bush.

"Violet, jobs don't grow on trees. Out here or anywhere. It sounds to me like you'd better contact someone at home and have them send you the money."

Her spirits sinking to her feet, she shook her head. There were several friends back in Amarillo who would gladly lend her money. But she doubted any of them had that much extra cash lying around the house. And even if they did, Violet wouldn't ask for such a loan.

"I don't—" *Have a home,* she very nearly blurted before she managed to catch herself. "There's not anyone to send me the money," she finished quickly.

"What about Grandpa? He has lots of money," Sam suggested, his expression all grins for having thought of such a sensible solution.

Without Violet even knowing it, a shutter fell over her face. "We can't…bother Grandpa with our troubles. He has plenty of his own."

Charlie's gaze went from mother to son and back again. She was obviously in a dilemma and a broken-down car was only a part of it. But that didn't surprise him. Women and trouble went hand in hand. If they didn't already have a problem, they would soon get themselves into one.

"What sort of job can you do?"

Violet's chin lifted. *What can you do?* The question grated on her like coarse sandpaper. She might look helpless and ignorant to him. But she wasn't. Neither was she lazy or afraid of work.

"I was working as a bookkeeper before, but..." she instinctively circled her arms around Sam and pulled him against her legs. "I'd prefer to do something where I could keep my son with me. But that's like wishing for rainbows every day of the year. I'll take whatever I can get and be glad for it."

She wasn't a Miss Goody Two-Shoes. Charlie could say that much for her. But she obviously wasn't using much common sense, either. What in hell kind of woman would head out with a small child across a lonely stretch such as Highway 380? And simply because they wanted an adventure!

He jerked his head toward his pickup truck, "Let's follow the wrecker. Once you get into town you can decide what you want to do, for tonight at least."

But tomorrow, Charlie told himself, she'd have to take care of herself. He was going to say goodbye to Violet O'Dell and head to the peace and quiet of the Pardee Ranch.

Chapter Two

The thirty-minute ride into Ruidoso gave Violet an opportunity to weigh her choices, but her mind was so weary it refused to think much further than a hot meal and cool, clean bed. And having Charlie Pardee sitting a short space away from her wasn't helping her state of mind, either. The man was far too distracting. All she wanted to do was look at him and think and wonder and imagine.

Violet didn't know what was the matter with her. Men were not on her Want list. As far as she was concerned, she never wanted to look at another man. Especially one who considered her too silly to get out of the rain, as this one seemed to. And he wasn't being the least bit inviting. So why was he striking a nerve in her?

Questions about the man were still nagging her when the outskirts of Ruidoso appeared ahead of them. The unexpected beauty of the town caught her attention, and for the next few minutes she pushed Charlie to the back of her mind and enjoyed the landscape flying by the pickup window.

Violet hadn't expected mountains to suddenly spring out of the desert. Especially mountains covered with tall, thick pine and cottonwood. The town itself was a blending of old and new. The shops and boutiques nestled along the winding streets appeared to cater to everyone from the cowboy to the snow skier to the art lover.

Ruidoso was beautiful, she decided as she breathed in the sharp, clean scent of evergreens. And from the looks of things it was going to be her temporary home for the next few weeks. It wasn't a thousand miles from Amarillo. But she couldn't let herself worry about that now. As long as no one back in Texas found her, she and Sam could survive. They were finally on their own, and Violet was determined to keep things that way.

At the garage Violet informed the mechanic she'd be contacting him in the next day or two to let him know what to do about repairing the motor. Once that was accomplished, she joined Charlie, who was waiting at the back of her vehicle.

"Does this town have a taxi service?" she asked as she handed him the key to the trunk.

"I think so." Without waiting for her reply, he opened the back of the car and motioned toward the bags and suitcases jammed in every crack and crevice of space. "You want everything out of here?"

Violet couldn't believe that less than twelve hours ago, she'd loaded the car with their things and driven away from Amarillo, away from the house that had been her home for the past seven years. Already it felt as if she and Sam had been traveling for days.

"I guess I will need most of them. We're going to be here for a while. Now what about the taxi?"

He placed an armload of bags on the ground at their feet, then straightened. If Charlie knew what was good for him he'd let her call a taxi and be done with her. But hellfire, he was already here. And Roy Pardee would never drive off from a stranded woman. In all good conscience, his son couldn't do it, either.

"What do you need a taxi for?"

She studied him with a guarded expression as though she was still trying to weigh the idea of trusting him.

"We're going to a motel," she told him. "And there's no need for you to bother driving us. We've already wasted enough of your time. I'm sure your family will be worrying about you."

Charlie's mouth twisted to a grim line. His parents weren't worried. As far as they knew he was still on the job in Texas. But he was beginning to worry about himself. It was time to let this woman and child go their own way, but something wouldn't quite let him.

"My folks aren't expecting me. I like to do things that way," he added when her brows arched with speculation. "You know, surprise them. Either way, Mom always cries when she sees me."

How wonderful, Violet thought, to have a family to go to, a mother and father who would always be glad to see you. But she wouldn't know about those things. Not since her mother had died ten years ago.

Her father, if he could be called such a thing, was still living back in Georgia. But Leroy Wilson had broken ties with them years ago. He'd wanted a bottle of vodka more than he'd wanted a family.

Violet glanced at the small watch, strapped to her wrist. Even though the summer sun was still burning high, it was nearing six-thirty in the evening.

"Well, this isn't getting either of us anywhere," she said, reaching into the trunk for more bags.

Charlie picked up those he'd earlier placed on the ground and carried them over to the bed of his truck.

"Where are we going now, Charlie?" Sam asked, hanging his head out the window.

The child had been waiting patiently in the cab of the truck. Charlie knew he had to be getting tired and hungry. But so far he'd been a little trooper. If Violet had been raising the child on her own since her husband died, he had to admit she'd been doing a good job.

Charlie paused by the open window. "I'm going to take you and your mommy to a motel."

Sam's little round face wrinkled with misgivings. "What's a motel?"

The question told Charlie the child had obviously never traveled before. At least not since he was old enough to remember things. "It's a place where you can rest and sleep."

"But I wanna eat," he quickly pointed out. "I don't wanna rest."

"Sam, don't argue. We'll eat as soon as we can," Violet told him, then to Charlie she asked, "Why are you putting my things in your truck? I told you we'd call a taxi."

"Are you always this contrary?" he asked sharply. Then, not allowing her the space of a breath to answer, he ordered, "Just get in the truck and I'll take you."

His demanding attitude would have normally infuriated Violet. But in this case she was more suspicious of the man than anything. A few hours ago he'd never laid eyes on her or her son. Their welfare or misfortune was none of his concern. Moreover, he didn't appear to be all that pleased to be bothered with them. So why didn't he go and leave them to their own business?

She tilted her head back to look at him. And from Violet's height that was a long way up.

"Are you one of those people who bring home poor strays you find on the street?" she asked him.

At one time in his life Charlie had been that sort of man.

And it was still his nature to help people. Until they wronged him. Then he could be as mean as a diamondback rattlesnake.

"The things I pick up off the street, Violet, I usually take to jail. You don't want to go there, do you?"

She supposed the cynical twist to his lips was supposed to be a smile. But Violet wasn't particularly warmed by it or his sarcastic brand of humor. It was too close to her fears to be funny.

"Not really," she answered tartly, then added, "I get the idea you'd rather be doing anything than what you're doing now, Charlie Pardee. I don't understand why you've taken my problem upon yourself."

He didn't understand it, either. But ever since the Lupé Valdez case, Charlie had not been himself. He felt constantly obliged to help and protect anyone and everyone. Even those that weren't his responsibility. He knew it was an impossible task, and he knew he was killing himself trying, but he couldn't make himself stop. Having Violet and Sam with him now was proof of that.

"For Pete's sake, I'm not making myself your social worker!" he said crossly. "I'm just going to drive you down the street. If you want to feel beholden to me for the rest of your life go ahead, I won't mind."

"You're making fun of me now."

He sighed and tried to shake away the frustration that was making him bite at this woman. "Not for anything would I do that."

For a Texas Ranger he was awfully loose, Violet thought, even brazen. But then maybe that was his style, his way of getting to people. Because he sure was getting to her. And the awful thing about it was he wasn't even trying.

"Okay, okay," she said, lifting her palms in a gesture of helpless surrender. "We'll accept a ride with you down the street."

Five minutes later, sitting behind the wheel of his truck, Charlie watched Violet enter the motel office. Beside him on the bench seat, Sam played with a miniature tractor his mother had fished from a bag in the back of the truck.

What was she going to do? Charlie asked himself for the hundredth time. Where would she find work, and what would she do with Sam, and what the hell did she mean by heading out on an adventure? On the surface the woman seemed sensible enough. In fact, she seemed nothing like a ditzy, half-cocked female just out for laughs and a joy ride.

Laughs. Charlie wasn't sure she knew how to laugh. So far he hadn't so much as seen a smile on her face. But then, to be fair, he couldn't remember the last time he'd really laughed himself. Perhaps they were birds of the same feather, Charlie decided. They'd both quit singing a long time ago.

His dark thoughts were suddenly broken by Sam's wheezy cough. He glanced down at the boy. "Are you getting sick, little guy?"

Sam shook his head. "Nope. I just have asthma sometimes. Mommy says it's those damn cattle pens that give it to me."

Charlie's lips twitched at Sam's innocent use of his mother's curse word. "Is that so? Did you live on a ranch?"

His nose wrinkled as he considered Charlie's question. "No. It wasn't a ranch. We lived with my grandpa in his house. And there's a stockyard down the road. But we're not gonna live there anymore. Mommy says there's a better place for us to live and there is, 'cause she's always right."

Her son had asthma, and she was looking for a better place for the two of them to live. Charlie supposed those two things weren't earth-shaking problems. But they were to someone with not even enough money to get their vehicle repaired.

But she and the boy weren't his problem, Charlie quickly reminded himself. No way, no how. He'd never laid eyes on the woman before today, and in a few more minutes he'd never see her again.

Anyway, she wasn't exactly poor or homeless, Charlie continued to argue with himself. Her clothes and the make of her car told him that much. More than likely, if she had problems, they were of her own making. She could find that better place for her and her son to live all by herself. She didn't need Charlie Pardee's help. And who the hell said he could help her, anyway? he asked himself bitterly. He hadn't been able to help Lupé.

The grim thought set off a buzz in his head as he watched her pay the man behind the counter several bills. If he'd only kept Lupé out of that motel. If he'd only taken her home with him instead of leaving her there that night. But like Violet, she'd been insistent that she could take care of herself.

The buzzing quickly turned to a roar, and the next thing Charlie knew he was inside the office, grabbing Violet by the arm.

"Get your money back," he ordered in a dangerously soft voice. "You're coming with me."

Her eyes wide with shock, Violet attempted to jerk loose from his hold. "What are you doing? I'm not going with you!"

"Yes, you are." He turned a cutting look on the man behind the counter. "Give her the money back. She's not staying here tonight."

The large man rocked back on his heels and eyed Charlie with a mocking smirk. "Look, mister, I don't want to get involved with your domestic quarrel. If you want to take the little lady home, take her. But the policy of this motel is no refunds.''

Violet's mouth fell open as her eyes darted from one man to the other. "I'm not going anywhere but to the room I just rented!'' she practically shouted at the two of them.

Ignoring her, Charlie pulled out his badge and flashed it to the proprietor. With eyes like steel and a voice to match, he said, "I'm changing your policy this time. Now give her the money!''

His feathers dampened by the prospect of tangling with a Ranger, the man counted the refund back onto the counter. Charlie snatched up the bills and pushed them into an open pocket on Violet's purse.

Because she didn't have much choice, she allowed him to lead her outside, but once they reached his pickup truck, Violet dug in her heels and refused to go any further.

"Okay, Ranger Pardee, what was that all about?'' she asked, her rising voice quivering with anger. "You just made a mess of everything! Now what am I going to do?''

He glanced down at her reddened cheeks and flashing green eyes. Even in her agitated state, she was the prettiest woman Charlie could ever remember seeing. But he told himself that had nothing to do with what he was about to say next. "Don't worry about it, Violet. You're coming home with me.''

Charlie didn't know what in hell had come over him. He was supposed to be on vacation. The next four weeks were his and his alone, to rest, sleep and eat whenever he wanted, to do absolutely nothing or whatever he felt like doing, whenever the urge struck him. He hadn't come back to New Mexico to wet-nurse a young woman and child!

Even now as Charlie drove east toward Hondo, he couldn't believe Violet and Sam were still with him. He didn't know how it had happened. One minute he'd been watching her pay a man for a motel room and the next he'd had her by the arm pushing her into his pickup.

Maybe his captain had been right a week ago when he'd said, "You need a long rest, Charlie. You're drained." For eighteen months Charlie had worked without a break, and nearly six months of that time had been spent on one intricate murder case involving a young Mexican woman. For a long time Charlie had tried to deny that the tragedy of Lupé Valdez had not affected him that deeply. He didn't *want* to believe her death had changed him. But now he wasn't so sure. He didn't take women he knew home with him. And especially home to the Pardee Ranch! What in hell was he going to do with her?

Violet shifted Sam's head to a more-comfortable position against her thigh and brushed his sweat-dampened hair away from his forehead. As soon as the Ranger had put the pickup truck back on the highway, her son had fallen into an exhausted sleep, and she felt very guilty because her plans had gone so awry. If the car hadn't broken down, the two of them would have been in Las Cruces by now, having a good hot meal and looking forward to a quiet night in a nice motel room. Instead she was driving to God-only-knew where with a man she'd met only a few hours ago. A Texas Ranger to boot!

Violet honestly wondered if the strain of the past months had finally broken her. Maybe losing Brent, then dealing with Rex had warped her ability to think sensibly. She couldn't think of any other reason why she would be putting herself and her son in the hands of a total stranger!

But there was something about Charlie Pardee, something beyond his muscles and stern demeanor that made Violet feel safe with him. He exuded confidence and self-assurance. He was a man who could take care of himself...and a woman, too, if the situation warranted it. So why did Violet get the shivers every time she looked at him? Why did she feel like she was headed to a lion's den, rather than a Ranger's haven?

"I haven't been to my cabin in over a year. I'm not sure what kind of condition it will be in. You should stay with my parents tonight," Charlie suggested a second time. "They have plenty of room. And if Dad being the sheriff is intimidating you, don't let it. Both my parents are hospitable people."

"I'm sure your parents are very nice. But I wouldn't feel right about imposing on them. I'm not even sure why I allowed you to bring Sam and me out here with you. I really think I'm losing my mind," she mumbled, then let out a small sigh.

Charlie could have voiced the same thing about himself, but he didn't. Instead, he glanced at her, then decided to voice the question uppermost in his thoughts. "Are you…having problems, Violet?"

Her head jerked up and her eyes found his profile in the waning light. "Problems? Of course I'm having problems! My car needs repairing, and I don't have the extra money to have it done."

His features hardened at her flip answer. "I wasn't referring to your car. I'm talking about…other things."

Violet's heart slowed to a fearful crawl. "What makes you ask something like that?"

His eyes still on the highway, he said curtly, "It's my job to know when things aren't exactly as they appear on the surface."

He didn't know about her surface beforehand or now. And he sure as heck wasn't going to find out what was underneath, Violet thought.

"Just because my vehicle broke down doesn't mean I'm a candidate for the psychiatrist's couch or a…jail cell."

"Defensive little thing, aren't you?" he countered.

Unconsciously her chin jutted forward. "Do you think if

I really needed to spill my guts, it would be to a Texas Ranger?''

"I am off duty," he drawled mockingly.

What would it be like, Violet wondered, to tell someone, anyone, all the fears, pressures and anger she'd lived with for so long now? She couldn't imagine the relief it might be to lay her head on Charlie Pardee's broad chest and pour it all out to him.

But Violet wasn't naive. She didn't have to be told that Charlie was never "off" duty. And the fear of Rex finding her through any remote channel would keep Violet's lips sealed forever. All that she'd left behind in Amarillo she would carry deep inside her, hold it to her and hope it had finally come to an end.

"Thanks for the offer of your ear, Charlie," she said as casually as she could manage. "But I wouldn't want to bore you."

A brief glance told him her face was as closed as her words. The suspicion she was hiding something should have warned him to turn the truck around and head back to Ruidoso. But Charlie wasn't known for always doing the sensible or right thing.

"Sam told me he had asthma."

She nodded. "Thankfully, it's only an occasional thing. That's one of the reasons I wanted to move from where we lived. It was very dusty and windy there. Not a good environment for a person with asthma."

Dusty and windy. In Texas that could mean anywhere east of the Brazos or as far north as Canada.

"He said his father had gone to heaven. Is that true?"

Violet wasn't at all sure Brent was wearing a halo. During the seven years she'd known him he'd turned from the loving man she'd first married to a stranger, someone she no longer wanted to know. But for Sam's sake she'd tried to soften the loss by assuring the child his father was with the angels.

Her eyes on the sleeping face of her child, she said, "Sam's father was killed in a plane crash. A light, single-engine. He flew into a thunderstorm. Wind shear severed the plane in two."

"He was a pilot?"

Violet nodded. "He got his pilot license because his job forced him to travel a lot."

"What did he do?"

She hesitated, then decided it would look very odd if she didn't say something. "He…uh, was a salesman for a meat company."

They were passing through a faint smattering of houses. One tiny building built close to the highway had a sign that read U.S. Post Office, Hondo, New Mexico.

Her brows lifted with wry amusement. The place wasn't large enough to be called a settlement, much less possess a United States Post Office, but maybe there were more people hidden in and around these desert mountains than she could see from Charlie's pickup truck.

"Were you raised in this area?" Violet found herself asking as he turned north onto a graveled dirt road.

"Until I was five my mother and I lived in Las Cruces. After that, we moved here, and my parents got married."

Violet knew she should keep her curiosity to herself. Tomorrow or the next day she and Sam would have to be finding a place of their own. She'd be saying goodbye to Charlie Pardee. The less she knew about the man the easier it would be to forget him.

"Your parents…weren't married when you were born?" she couldn't help asking.

He had slowed the truck considerably since they had left the main highway. Through the dusky light outside the windshield, she could see clumps of choya and sage and a few scrubby piñon pine dotting the hills rising around them. Violet had never traveled this far west before, and its stark beauty mesmerized her as much as the man behind the wheel.

"No," he answered. "When my mother was pregnant with me, she left here thinking my dad was obligated to marry someone else. And my dad didn't know about me. A few years later my mother decided to return to Hondo Valley to be with her family. It was then my father learned he had a son, and in the process my parents realized how much they still loved each other."

Her gaze slipped over his strong face. "That's quite a romantic story," she murmured.

To Charlie's annoyance, he felt a blush sting his cheeks. He was a grown man who'd seen and heard everything. He didn't think there was anything that could embarrass him. But somehow Violet had managed to leave him feeling like an awkward teenager for relating his parents' history.

"I wouldn't call it romantic," he muttered. "For a while it was hell for both of them."

His sharp cynicism shouldn't have surprised Violet. She had already decided he wasn't the most cheerful of men. Yet he did seem to be a man who had deep values. She wouldn't have taken him for a man to mock love or romance. But then he could have been burned by a lover or wife and never gotten over it. And that idea unsettled her far more than his hard-bitten attitude.

"Have you...ever been married, Charlie?"

He felt the warmth of that damn blush on his face deepen, suffusing his face with unaccustomed heat. "No," he said curtly. "I'm not the marrying kind."

Her brows arched, but other than that she made no remark to his answer. Charlie wondered what she was thinking and why she'd asked the personal question in the first place. She was not a woman looking for a man. He'd come to that conclusion within minutes after meeting her. So what was she looking for, he asked himself. Money? Security? A hiding place?

"How long had you been married when your husband was killed?" he asked.

Violet carefully kept her eyes on the darkening landscape. She didn't like thinking about her marriage to Brent. It reminded her of how foolish and vulnerable she'd once been. And how she could never be the loving, trusting woman who'd first married him.

"Six years," she said quietly.

Charlie mulled this over. "That's a hell of a thing to have happen."

Guilt coursed its way through Violet. Charlie believed she'd been a grieving, devastated widow. And maybe she had been, to a certain degree. Heaven knew she'd never wanted Brent to die. She'd simply wanted him out of her and Sam's life. When she'd filed for divorce, she'd had no way of knowing a week later her husband's plane was going to crash.

"It was," she agreed. "But time has helped us to adjust. We're making it okay."

From the closed expression on her face, Charlie figured she'd either loved her husband very much or hated the very sight of him. And he was angry with himself for wanting to know which.

She cast him a sparing glance. "Have you been a Texas Ranger for long?"

"Seven years."

He must have become a lawman at a very early age, Violet decided. She doubted he'd seen his thirtieth birthday yet.

"You must like it," she mused aloud.

His lips twisted sardonically. Charlie never thought about

whether he liked being a Ranger. He just was one. He couldn't imagine himself being anything but a Ranger.

"My dad has been the sheriff of Lincoln County for nearly thirty years. Being a man of the law is a way of life for him. And me, too."

A way of life. Violet didn't know what her way of life was. She wasn't sure she'd ever had one. She'd always been a daughter or a wife. She'd gone from living at home with her parents straight into marriage. She'd never really been out on her own, with the chance to be Violet Wilson or Violet O'Dell.

Sighing, Violet gazed down at Sam, who was still sound asleep in spite of the roughening road and the jostling of the truck. "I hope I can let Sam choose his own path as he grows up. I want him to make good decisions, but I don't want to push him to be something he isn't comfortable with."

"I don't know what it's like to have a child, and I probably won't ever know," Charlie replied, "but I expect letting loose of the reins is the hardest part of raising one."

He wasn't the marrying sort, and he didn't expect to have children. Violet understood there were plenty of men in the world who didn't want families. But somehow the idea of Charlie Pardee living alone for the rest of his life just didn't fit.

The road made a wide bend around another bald hill, and Violet leaned forward as the vague outline of a house and trees appeared in the distance.

"Is that your cabin?" Violet asked. "It looks more like a house to me."

"House. Cabin. Whatever you want to call it, there it is. If we're lucky, the electricity will be on."

Violet couldn't believe the house had electricity. This must be the darkest place she'd ever seen. For as far as she could see there were no houses with lights or any sign of civilization. The horizon held nothing but desert hills and a rising crescent moon.

Charlie parked in front of the house and instructed Violet to wait in the truck until he unlocked the door and made sure the power was on.

In a matter of moments a light flared in the window, and then he was back, lifting her son off her lap. "I'll carry Sam. Follow me and watch your step. The ground is rocky out here."

On the way to the house Violet drank in the utter quiet, the soft breeze scented with sage and piñon, and the moonlight slanting silver rays across the yard. She'd never lived in the country before. Nor had she ever thought she'd want to, but she could see why Charlie considered this place as coming home. There was an inviting serenity about it all.

Just inside the door Charlie turned to her. "I'm going to put Sam on the couch for now. I'm not sure whether the beds are made up with clean sheets."

"Of course. Thank you for carrying him. He's getting to be quite a load." She watched him lay the child gently down on a couch covered with a blanket in a bright, Southwestern design.

For a man who as yet had no children or plans to have any, he seemed adept at handling them. Maybe he had dated a woman with children, she surmised. Or maybe things just came naturally to Charlie Pardee.

Straightening to his full height, Charlie looked at her. She was standing in the middle of the small room, her hands linked tightly in front of her. No doubt she was probably wondering what she'd gotten herself into, by coming out to this secluded place with a man she didn't know. And if she wasn't a little bit scared, she ought to be, he thought grimly.

"Well," he said, then roughly cleared his throat. "I'm going to unload the truck. When I'm finished, we'll find something to eat. I brought a few groceries with me, and there should be some things in the cupboards. Do you know how to cook?''

Violet's gaze wandered curiously around the room. It was small but neat, with everything in its place. The furniture was sturdy, wood-framed pieces with cushions covered in copper-colored hopsacking. Heavy, unbleached muslin draped across a pair of wide-paned windows. There were several Navajo woven rugs on the floor, the head of a stuffed mule deer on the wall, along with a gun rack stacked with an assortment of high-powered rifles. It was obviously a man's house, yet it was warm and homey. And as solid and strong as Charlie Pardee himself.

Eventually Violet's eyes settled back on his strong face, and as she looked at him she wondered why fate had brought her to a man who had the power to hurt her the most.

''I can find my way around a kitchen, Ranger Pardee.''

Chapter Three

"Hamburgers, hot dogs or lunch meat." Charlie pulled each food item from an ice chest, carelessly tossed the packages on the tabletop, then walked over to a wall lined with varnished pine cabinets. The countless number of canned goods displayed on the shelves reminded him of just how long it had been since he'd been home. "The choices here are soup, chili, tamales and refried beans."

"Sam and I aren't particular eaters," Violet assured him from her seat at the little farm table. "We'll eat anything. Just tell me what you want and I'll prepare it."

Even though he'd asked her if she could cook, Charlie hadn't really expected her to. She wasn't exactly a guest, but she wasn't hired help, either. She wasn't a relative or even a girlfriend. He really didn't know how the hell to treat her. "I didn't bring you out here to make you my slave."

For the first time since they had met on the side of the highway, Violet gave him a little smile. It was the most knowing, provocative, female expression he'd ever seen on any woman, and as his eyes settled on her lips, he felt something stir deep in his gut.

"I don't see a whip in your hand," she told him. "I'd like the chance to compensate for all this trouble you've gone to. I really feel like Sam and I shouldn't be here."

He was inclined to agree with her. She and the boy shouldn't be here. He was a man who enjoyed his own company. Especially when he was in a black mood, and lately he'd been in a lot of those. Besides, a woman and child could only mean trouble he didn't need. Yet in spite of all his misgiving, she was here and he found himself more and more intrigued with her.

Propping a thigh on the corner of the table, he folded his arms against his chest. His assessing gaze roamed her face. "Are you a jinx? Should I be worried the roof or something will fall in on us?"

Violet had been around big, muscular men before. For the past two years she'd worked in a place where men of all shapes and sizes came and went. She was used to them and rarely gave any of them a second glance. But there was something about Charlie that made her heart beat out of rhythm every time her eyes touched him. She didn't know if the breadth of his shoulders, the thickness of his chest, the sandy hair flopping defiantly over one eye or merely the deep, resonating sound of his voice was affecting her. The only thing she did know was that her strong reaction to him was very unsettling to her peace of mind.

Desperate to lengthen the distance between them, Violet rose from her chair and walked over to the groceries scattered across the counter. "With the luck I've had today it looks as though I'm a jinx."

With narrowed eyes, he watched her quickly set about unpacking the last sack of groceries. "Violet, you can't imagine what sort of trouble you might have gotten into if I hadn't come along."

She supposed as a lawman he'd seen plenty of heinous crimes against women, and he'd naturally think of the worst scenario happening.

"I suppose I should look at it that way," she conceded. But had she been lucky? Violet wondered. She wasn't so sure. Each time she looked at him, she got the feeling she'd run from a storm and straight into a wildfire.

A few minutes later Violet began to prepare sandwiches for their supper. While she worked, Charlie went to the bedroom to check the beds. Both mattresses had been stripped of sheets, so he found two clean sets from a small linen closet, tossed one set on his own bed, then carried the other to the guest bedroom.

He was slipping the puckered corners of the sheet over the mattress when Violet appeared in the doorway. She immediately walked to the head of the bed and grabbed one end of the pale blue muslin. "Let me help you," she offered. "It's always easier when two make a bed."

"My parents come over and stay here at the cabin sometimes just for the heck of it. Mom must have taken the sheets to wash them," Charlie explained, then glanced across the bed at her.

Other than his sister Caroline and his cousins Anna and Ivy, he'd never had a woman out here to his cabin before. Having Violet in the small bedroom with him made Charlie more aware than ever that she was a beautiful woman and he was a man who'd gone without female company for a long, long time.

His thoughts must have shown on his face because Violet suddenly straightened away from the bed and took a couple of wary steps backward. Crossing her arms over her plump little breasts, she said, "The sandwiches are ready whenever you are. I also opened the carton of milk and poured a small glass for Sam. I hope you don't mind."

Down through the years Charlie had provoked a lot of

reactions from women. He could say without conceit nearly all of them had been positive. Try as he might he could never remember any woman being so leery of angering him. Had he become that hard and forbidding, or had Violet lived with a husband that had been less than loving?

The dark thought left Charlie's voice rougher than usual. "The kid can drink the whole carton. I'll be getting whatever I need when I drive back into Ruidoso."

Deciding he was becoming far too aware of her sweet scent, soft body and shadowy green eyes, he quickly whipped the flat sheet in the air and allowed it to settle over the double bed.

Violet ventured forward once again and tucked the sheet under her side of the mattress. "You will be going back to Ruidoso tomorrow, won't you?" she asked.

If he had any sense at all, he'd take Violet and Sam right back to Ruidoso in the morning. But he was sick of driving, of traveling, and most of all not being able to stay in one spot for more than five hours at a time.

Shrugging he said, "I don't know. I haven't decided when I'll go back into town."

Violet's heart stilled as she watched his lean, tanned hand smooth the blue sheet over the end of the bed. She never would have agreed to come out here for more than one night. He should have told her his intentions!

"What do you mean, you don't know? Sam and I have to get back. We can't stay here!"

Hysteria tinged the last of her words and Charlie glanced at her. From the expression on her face, he might as well have announced an atomic bomb was sitting under his little summer cabin. He felt his patience rapidly slipping.

"Why can't you stay here?" he countered. "Your car is out of commission. What could you do in town?"

What did the man think she was going to do here? Violet wondered wildly. They were out in the middle of nowhere.

"Try to find a job," she answered, her voice conveying how ridiculous she considered his question.

"How?"

Moving from the back side of the bed, he came to stand a couple of short steps away from her. His thumbs were looped into the front pockets of his jeans. "Your car isn't running. If you hired a taxi to drive you around for job interviews, you'd only be wasting money you obviously need. And Ruidoso is far too spread out to walk it. Besides, what would you do with Sam while you went job hunting?"

She threw up her hands in disgust. "The way you make it sound, I might as well go jump off a cliff and put myself out of this misery."

For the first time since she'd met him, his face turned dark and rigid with anger. He stepped closer, and Violet's heart began to pound rapidly as his fingers wrapped tightly around her upper arm.

"If you're going to talk like a fool I don't want you around here!" he said sharply.

The harshness of his words hurt, more than angered, Violet. Since she'd met him on the side of the highway she hadn't exactly been amiable, but up until this moment, she'd believed him to be a fair, considerate man, a person who might actually care what happened to her and Sam. Dear Lord, she'd let her imaginations stray into left field this time.

Stiffening her spine and lifting her chin, she tried her best to hide the awful embarrassment she was feeling at imposing on this man's privacy.

"I was pretty sure you didn't want me around here before you ever left Ruidoso," she said coolly. "I don't know why you insisted Sam and I traipse out here with you. You don't know us, and I really doubt you want to get to know us. Now you're stuck with us. And I feel awful and you—"

Violet's words were suddenly smothered to a shocked moan as Charlie's head dipped and his lips captured hers. Stunned motionless by the intimate contact, Violet tried to shut down her senses, too. She tried to tell herself she didn't want Charlie Pardee's kiss on her lips any more than she'd wanted Brent's after their marriage had technically ended. But her brain, or maybe it was her heart, refused to cooperate. By the time Charlie lifted his head, Violet was on the verge of swooning straight into his arms.

"Why did you do that?" she whispered huskily.

His heart beating like a drum in his chest, Charlie's blue eyes swept over her pink cheeks and puffy lips. Damn it all, kissing her had been the last thing he'd planned on doing. But then she'd started that rambling tirade which hadn't made one lick of sense to him and he'd lost all control.

"To shut you up," he answered, his breaths still coming short and fast.

She glared at him in disbelief.

He didn't wait for her to make any sort of remark. He lit into her with a voice as rock hard as his face. "Over the course of a year I see more murder victims than I want to see. None of those people had a choice to keep living. Someone else decided to take it away. And you—"

"Are you crazy or something?" she cut in hotly. "When I said jump off a cliff, I didn't mean it literally! And if you'll recall, you were the one listing all the reasons why I should wring my hands together and cry. Well, let me tell you something, Mister Texas Ranger, I'm not a weak, sniveling person who crumbles at the first sign of trouble. I've been through more than you'll ever know, and never once have I considered copping out on myself or my son or anyone. And furthermore, I don't let just anybody kiss me! Got that?"

She needn't worry about a repeat performance, Charlie

thought. Kissing Violet O'Dell had left him feeling as if he'd been whammed on the head with a nine-pound hammer.

"Yeah, I got it," he muttered. "And maybe we should go eat before we have any more of these misunderstandings."

Violet had never heard of a kiss labeled as a misunderstanding. In her opinion the word didn't begin to describe the storm that had rushed through her the moment his lips had touched hers. She still felt the need to draw in several cleansing breaths and give herself a hard mental shake.

"I'll go wake Sam," she told him, then shot out of the room on shaky legs.

The meal of sandwiches was a solemn affair. Sam's nap had left him quiet and groggy. As for Violet she felt as unwanted and in the way as an ant at a picnic. As she forced the ham and cheese past her tight throat, she wished a thousand times she'd never allowed Charlie to bully her into coming out here. It had been a drastic mistake, and if he'd had a regular telephone available, she would call a taxi as soon as she cleaned the supper table. But the only phone she'd seen anywhere was the cellular in his truck. And he'd disconnected it shortly after they had arrived at the cabin.

A short while later as Violet sat on the side of the tub, supervising Sam's bath, he asked, "Mommy, are we gonna sleep here at Charlie's house tonight?"

"Yes. For tonight," she answered.

The child plopped the sopping washcloth on top of his head, then squinted his eyes and giggled as rivulets of water rushed over his face.

Violet smiled gently at his playful antics. It was a relief to see her son didn't appear to be the least bit traumatized or confused by all that had happened today. He seemed to feel as much at home here as he had in the house they had shared with Brent's father.

"Tomorrow when it gets light, can I go outside and play?" he asked. "Do you think Charlie might play with me?"

Violet didn't want to think about Charlie Pardee. The man had more sides to him than a pair of dice. Worse than that, he was a lawman. Just being in the same house with him was like playing with fire.

"You might go outside for a little while if it's not too hot," she told Sam. "But I'm sure Charlie will be too busy to play."

One thing Violet could say about Brent—he'd been a good father to their son. Though his job had required him to travel often, whenever he was home he'd always made a point of spending time with Sam. Even when their marriage had turned sour, his love for Sam had never wavered. Violet supposed that was the main reason why she'd tried to hold their marriage together for the last year before he'd died. Sam had needed his father, and Brent had always been there for him. She hadn't been able to bring herself to tear them apart with a divorce.

In the past months Violet was aware her son missed and needed the male companionship Brent had provided. And now that the two of them had left Amarillo, she'd taken him away from his grandfather, too. A part of Violet felt guilty about the separation. The man was the only close relative either of them had left. But he was not the sort of male influence she wanted for Sam. On the contrary, she prayed her son would not grow up to be like the O'Dell men before him.

"Mommy, when are we gonna get to our new home? Is it a long way from here?"

Sam's questions stabbed her heart. A stable home in a clean, quiet little town was something she desperately wanted to give her son. He deserved it. He shouldn't have to suffer just because his father had died or his grandfather was a greedy, evil man.

"I'm not sure, darling. But I promise we'll find it soon. And then you can have a swing set and a sand box and maybe even a cat or dog."

"Oh boy! I want a dog. A big one like Rin Tin Tin."

A faint smile tilted Violet's lips as she leaned over and kissed the top of Sam's wet head. "You'd better finish your bath now, honey. We'll talk some more about the dog later."

By the time Sam was dressed in his pajamas and she'd helped him brush his teeth, his eyes were growing droopy once again. Violet put him to bed in the room where Charlie had kissed her. But she tried to put the ridiculous way she'd reacted to the man out of her mind. She had much more serious things to think about. Like how she was going to get her car going and move on before Rex could find her.

"Will you tell me a story, Mommy? Just a little one?" Sam pleaded as Violet tucked the sheet around him.

Sitting on the side of the bed, she took his small hand in hers. "I really think it's time for you to go to sleep. You've had a long day, young man."

"But I want to hear about the dog," he protested. "Can we name him Mike and get him a doghouse to sleep in?"

"Sure we can. And we'll get him a collar and put his name on it so everyone will know he's Mike."

Sam's sleepy eyes glowed with anticipation. "And can I take him for a walk and make him fetch?"

Violet's smile was full of love as she gazed down at her son. When Sam had been born, she'd been the happiest woman alive. She had all she'd ever dreamed and hoped for. A husband who adored her and a baby to complete their family.

But her happiness hadn't meant to be forever, she thought sadly as her thoughts slipped back in time. By the time Sam had turned three, Violet discovered Brent had been unfaithful during one of his business travels. Of course, she had been shattered by his betrayal. But because she loved him, she'd wanted desperately to believe him when he promised it had been a terrible mistake on his part and would never happen again.

Eventually she had forgiven him. But deep down her trust in him had died. Whether Brent had sensed the change in her and resented it or whether he'd simply grown restless again, Violet would never know. Whatever the reason, his philandering started all over again, and because of it, their marriage began to crumble.

Her gaze slipped back to her son as she tried to shake away the depressing memories. Heartache or not, having Sam had made her marriage to Brent worthwhile. Other than her mother, her son was the only person to ever love her completely and unconditionally. She would do anything she had to do to keep him safe and happy.

"Yes, you can take him for walks and let him fetch," she answered Sam's question. "But first you have to teach your dog how to follow a leash and to return whatever you send him after, like a ball or stick."

"Oh I will, Mommy. Mike will be really smart and everywhere I go, he'll go, too!"

"That sounds nice." She leaned over and kissed his forehead, then nuzzled her nose against his cheek. "And tomorrow we'll start looking for our home. "I promise."

"Goodnight, Mommy."

She turned out the light and slipped quietly from the bedroom. After a quick glance in the living room and kitchen, she decided Charlie must have gone to bed while she'd been giving Sam a bath. That was more than okay with her. She wasn't company who expected or needed the attention from a host. As far as she was concerned she wished she could avoid Charlie Pardee altogether. If there was any way she could walk safely out of here with her son, she wouldn't hesitate to hit the road.

Deciding a bit of night air was what she needed to soothe her ruffled nerves, Violet stepped out onto the front porch, then immediately wished she hadn't.

Charlie's tall frame was tilted back in a straight, wooden chair. His booted feet were propped on the porch banister. The moment he heard her footfall, he turned his head in her direction.

"Sorry I disturbed you," she said quietly, "I didn't know you were out here."

He continued to study her, standing there in the shadows. She wasn't disturbing him, Charlie thought. At least, not in the way she was thinking.

Hating to appear as unsociable as he felt, he flexed a hand toward the chair next to him. "Since you're already out here, you might as well sit down."

She eyed the roped-bottomed chair. It was only a small space away from the man. Maybe it was silly of her, but she didn't want to get that close to him. She didn't want to be tempted to look at his handsome face, to wonder what it would be like to be kissed by him again, kissed as if she were a woman he really wanted.

The whole idea sent a shiver down her spine, but she forced herself to walk to the chair and plop down as if he were no more than a pesky brother.

"It is much cooler now that night has fallen," she said, lifting the heavy swathe of dark hair off her neck. "Sometimes when it's hot like today, I think I should take Sam to a cool state. Northern California might be nice."

Charlie's gaze followed the slim, elegant line of her neck, then down to the thrust of her breasts. She was a small woman but every curve was full and perfect, just made for a man to hold. Yet he tried his best not to think about that. From past experience he knew that he and women didn't mix. Texas Rangers were married to their state and the law that protected it.

"Have you lived there before?" he asked.

Violet's sigh was wistful. "I've never been to California. But I've read about it. The northern part has pines and mountains and lots of snow in the wintertime."

One corner of his mouth lifted mockingly. She sounded as if she were searching for the end of the rainbow. Didn't she know paradise didn't exist?

"Ruidoso's elevation is seven thousand feet, so it gets plenty of snow. And in case you weren't looking, it has pines and mountains, too."

Violet could have told him it wasn't necessarily a place in California she needed or wanted. Under different circumstances she would probably find Ruidoso perfect for her and Sam to settle down in. But the town just wasn't far enough away from Amarillo for her peace of mind.

"I noticed it was very beautiful…but…I'll be moving on once my car is fixed."

Charlie turned his gaze back to the low, rolling hills in the near distance. He knew this land and every part of the Pardee Ranch as well as he knew the back of his hand. This place was as much a part of him as the very beat of his heart. It was home. He couldn't imagine how it would feel to be like Violet, wandering, searching and alone. But wasn't he like her? an insistent little voice inside his head whispered back at him. Hadn't he really come back to New Mexico for relief, for a place to dump the blackness in his heart?

"California isn't necessarily the end of the rainbow, if that's what you've got in your head."

He wouldn't ever know what she had in her head, she

thought. She frowned at him. "I'm not looking for a pot of gold. Money isn't what I want."

He grunted with mocking disbelief. "You were just whining earlier that you had to find a job to get enough money to fix your car. You're lying if you say you don't want money. Everybody wants it."

She took a deep breath and tried not to let his attitude rile her. Even though this man was perturbing, he was helping her. She had to keep that uppermost in her mind. "You work as a Ranger just for the money?"

"It's a job. It's the way I pay my bills."

Once again he'd avoided answering her question about his feelings on being a lawman. But Violet wasn't going to point this out to him. The fact that he was so closed on the subject told her far more than he realized. Charlie Pardee wasn't an altogether contented man.

She didn't make any sort of reply, and after several minutes of awkward silence had passed, Charlie glanced at her.

"Have you ever lived in California?" From the drawl in her voice, he very much doubted it. But it was possible she'd been there for a brief time. Why he was curious, he didn't know.

Violet shook her head. "I was raised in Georgia and lived there until I married my late husband and moved to Texas. I grew up where cotton and peanuts were raised."

"You don't...have family there now?"

She didn't answer, and his blue eyes continued to watch her every reaction. She released the heavy curtain of hair, and it rippled back against her neck. Her mouth was grim, her eyes sad.

"My father still lives there. But we're estranged. He's an alcoholic."

Charlie was surprised by her bluntly spoken admission. So far, she'd been very closemouthed. He'd never expected her to open up to him this much. Especially after the way he'd kissed her. She'd really been put out over that, and he hoped she was a woman who could forget easily. The last thing he wanted was to have her thinking he had designs on her.

Hell, he didn't want or need any woman, Charlie told himself. To get tangled up with a widow and her child would be crazy. True, he shouldn't have kissed her. But it had been an impulsive thing on his part. He had no intention of repeating it.

"What about your mother? Is she still in Georgia?"

Violet's gaze dropped to her lap. To this day it hurt to remember her mother was gone, that she could no longer pick up the phone and hear her gentle voice or walk into a room and see her smile. Betty Wilson had been a hard-working, sensible woman whose only fault had been loving her family too much.

"My mother died about ten years ago. She had heart disease and needed a transplant, but we were poor and had no way to raise the money. Some of the local townspeople eventually tried to help by putting on fundraisers. We'd finally gathered enough together to get Mother's name put on a waiting list, but it was too late."

Her mother had died and left her with an alcoholic father. God, how fortunate he'd been to have had two wonderful parents all these years, Charlie told himself. "Do you have siblings?" he asked.

"No. I was an adopted child."

An emotion he couldn't describe settled over him like the chill of a misty cloud, and Charlie wished he'd kept his question to himself. He'd often feared being a lawman was hardening him, making him indifferent. A lawman couldn't take all the ugly things he saw to heart. He had to remain impersonal or he'd go insane. So why was he getting a need to make things better for Violet O'Dell? Because he was still trying to atone for Lupé's death. Well as far as he was concerned nothing would ever do that.

Unsettled by his thoughts, he rose from the chair, paced across the length of the porch, then came back to stand in front of Violet. "I overheard you and Sam talking earlier when he was in the bathtub," he said. "You don't really have a certain place to go to, do you?"

She plucked at the hem of her shorts, and Charlie's eyes were drawn to her legs. The urge to slide his fingers over the smooth calves was a strong one. But incredibly, the desire to see a smile on her face was even greater.

"No," she answered. "We really have set out on an adventure, and I'm not exactly sure where it will end."

Charlie wanted to jerk her out of the chair, take her by the shoulders and shake her. He wanted to yell how foolish and dangerous it was for her to be traveling alone with a child, that she shouldn't be on an adventure, she should be home. But did she have a home? And if he asked her would he get the truth?

"The way Sam talked he's never had a pet before."

Violet looked out at the quiet night. She'd never been in such an isolated place, and she'd expected to find it frightening, but as she looked out at the sage and cactus and scrubby piñon tipped with silver moonlight, she thought she'd never seen anything more beautiful.

"Before now I didn't think he was old enough to know how to treat or take care of a pet. But he's matured these past six months, so I'm going to see what I can do about getting him a dog." A vague smile crossed her face. "I'm not so sure about getting a German Shepherd, though. We might have to start with something a bit smaller."

The itch to question her further clawed at Charlie's insides. The man in him, not the Ranger wanted to know why she was running. Oh, yes, he knew she was on the run from something. Whether it be a lover or the law, or simply herself, he could see her looking behind her with fear in her eyes. Yet he had no right to interrogate her. She wasn't a criminal. Or so he doubted. Whether she'd had a home or was running because she didn't was something she'd have to tell him on her own. He wasn't going to pry it out of her.

"Do you have any siblings?" she asked.

Charlie had been so deep in thought about her it took a moment to switch his attention to himself. "I have a sister six years younger than me. Last year she graduated with a degree in art. Now she lives in Santa Fe. You know, the mystical place that calls to writers and artists," he said with wry fondness.

"She sounds interesting. Does she paint?"

"She can paint beautifully. But she makes her living designing jewelry. Particularly silver jewelry."

"Do you see her very often?"

There was a faint wistful note in Violet's voice, and he was almost ashamed to tell her he only saw Caroline a few times a year. She obviously thought he was blessed to have a sibling. And he was. But he was human, and more often than not he took his blessings for granted.

"Whenever my job allows me to come home on holidays. Caroline is always home then."

"Is she married?"

Charlie grunted with wry amusement. "Caroline married? She wishes. She's a fiery redhead like my mom. She hasn't found a man brave enough to take her on. But she's only twenty-three. That's too young to get married, anyway."

Violet glanced at him briefly, then turned her eyes on the distant hills. "I'm twenty-four and I feel like an old woman."

Though she appeared to be very young physically, Charlie was inclined to believe she really did feel old. She looked at him with eyes far older than her years, eyes that had already seen more than many did in a lifetime.

"Violet, I...earlier in the bedroom...it's not like me to jump to conclusions over an innocent remark." He forced himself to look at her, and he felt a jolt deep inside as his eyes caught the green shimmer of her gaze staring back at him. "And grabbing you like I did...you'll do well not to read anything into that."

She swallowed as an unexpected lump of emotion filled her throat. She wasn't looking for a man. After the damage Brent had wrought on her heart, she didn't know if she could ever trust another man or even if she wanted to try. But to hear Charlie dismiss their kiss as though it had been nothing to him, cut her deep.

"If you're trying to apologize, Charlie, there's really no need. I realize this has to be unsettling to have a woman and child in your cabin on your first night home. And I didn't figure that was really you kissing me, anyway," she lied.

His eyes narrowed on her face. "Who did you think it was?"

One of her shoulders lifted and fell and she ducked her head as heat filled her cheeks. "That was just your frustration coming out," she murmured.

He leaned his hip against the porch railing and crossed his arms over his chest. "You're wrong, Violet. It *was* a little bit of me coming out." He studied her down-bent head. She might have been married for six years and borne a child, but she still seemed terribly naive in some ways.

"I get the idea you think I'm not like other men because I'm a Texas Ranger. That's where you're wrong. Men are men under any guise. And deep down all of us are selfish. That's just the way we're made. We can't help it."

Her expression turned to comic disbelief. "Why are you saying such things to me? Are you afraid I'm going to let my imagination run away with me? That I'll get to thinking you kissed me because you wanted to?'' She let out a scoffing laugh. ''Charlie, I might be young in years, but I wasn't born yesterday. I'm not getting those sorts of ideas about you. Believe me, as soon as I can get out of your hair, I'll be glad to go.''

He was getting the urge to kiss her again, to reach over and pluck her from the chair, pull her into his arms and ravish her soft lips. Violet thought it was frustration and not really him that had compelled him to kiss her. But right this moment it felt like the urge was pure Charlie Pardee.

''Violet,'' he started to say, then stopped and heaved out a heavy breath. ''I'm not telling you all this just to hear myself talk! When you leave here you can't go around trusting the first man who comes along!''

He was actually angry! She couldn't believe him. ''I have no intention of doing such a thing.''

''But you might be tempted. Especially when things are going rough and you start to have doubts about making it on your own. You might be tempted to lean on a man…to let him take care of you. And he just might be the wrong man.

Her head swung from side to side. ''Do I look stupid or something? Or do you give this sort of lecture to all the women you know?''

He made a little growling sound in his throat. ''No. I don't normally preach to the females I come in contact with. But I know…without you having to tell me…that you have problems.''

She opened her mouth to deny his speculation, but he held up his hand and barged on without giving her the chance. ''Maybe your trouble wasn't over a man. But then, maybe it was.'' His eyes flicked insolently over her. ''From the looks of you, I'd bet everything I own that you left Texas because of a man.''

What was he seeing when he looked at her, a jezebel, a siren, a lady of the night? Love or sex had nothing to do with her flight from Texas, and the very idea that he thought it did enraged her.

"Then you'd lose," Violet whispered fiercely. "Not that it's any of your business!"

She was about to rise from the chair when Charlie suddenly grabbed her arm and jerked her to her feet.

"What are you—" The rest of her question was lost as she landed with a thump against his chest, and the breath whooshed out of her.

"I'm making it my business," he muttered, his hand snatching a grip on her chin. "Somebody needs to shock some sense into you!"

Sense? What sort of sense was this, she wanted to scream at him, but he didn't give her the chance. His head bent, and before she could draw a breath his lips were hovering above hers, turning her heart into a frantic runaway.

"I don't think you realize the trouble you could get yourself into. With me...or any man," he whispered roughly.

Any man could never make her feel like this, she thought wildly. Just the idea of feeling his lips against hers made her head reel. But as for trouble, she'd grown up with it, lived with and was still trying to get out of it.

"Trouble is my middle name, Ranger Pardee. But it isn't your problem," she said, hating the sound of her breathy voice and the thrill she was feeling at being so close to him.

She was right. It wasn't his problem. And he should load her up right now, this very minute, and haul her into Ruidoso. But the kid was inside asleep. It would be cruel to jerk him out of bed, Charlie argued with himself.

And anyway, he knew he'd never be able to leave her at some motel and drive away. She reminded him too much of another young woman who'd sworn she was capable of taking care of herself. She hadn't been. And neither was Violet O'Dell. That's why he was going to have to do it for her. At least for a little while.

"I'm a Texas Ranger. My job is dealing with trouble before or after it happens. And it looks like right now my job is you."

Shocked by his touch and all that he was saying, Violet stared helplessly up into his blue eyes until his face grew so close it was nothing but a blur. And then it was too late to tell herself to push him away, to convince herself she didn't want to be in his arms. He was kissing her again. And this time it didn't feel a bit like anger. It felt all man.

Chapter Four

The morning air was cool with just a hint of breeze, and Violet sighed with appreciation as she lifted her coffee cup to her lips. She'd been sitting on the porch for at least thirty minutes, savoring the quiet of the desert while waiting for the two males inside the house to wake.

Not that she was looking forward to facing Charlie this morning. After that kiss on the porch last night, Violet wished she could hide under a rock with one of those horned toads he'd been telling Sam about yesterday.

Even though she'd finally managed to gather enough of her senses together to end the kiss, as far as she was concerned it had been too little, too late. Her lips had already told him how much she liked the taste of him.

As for Charlie thinking he needed to take care of her, she didn't know where he'd gotten the idea. And once she'd managed to pull herself out of his arms, she hadn't waited around to ask him. She'd run straight to the bedroom, slipped into bed with Sam and prayed for sleep to blot out her churning thoughts. Too bad it had taken hours for that to happen, and even then her eyes had popped back open long before dawn.

Violet was still trying to put last night and Charlie out of her mind when the far-off hum of a vehicle caught her attention. She didn't believe there were other roads branching off the one coming here to the house. From what Charlie had told her, this whole section of land belonged solely to the Pardees. They didn't lease any of it, and their only neighbors lived several more miles on down the highway.

She had just about decided to go wake Charlie and warn him that someone was coming when a blue pickup truck topped a rise just to the south. Violet watched the truck and the following plume of dust as it curved its way through the juniper and sage and finally pulled to a halt a few feet away from the porch.

Even more surprising to Violet than the idea of someone calling not long after sunrise was the sight of the woman driver climbing to the ground. She was tall and slender and wore blue jeans and a sleeveless white top. Her hair was a fiery copper color and pulled atop her head in a mass of loose curls. She was more than just attractive. She was sexy and carried herself with an air of self-confidence that Violet was still searching for.

As she approached the steps she eyed Violet as if finding a woman there was as unexpected as snow in July. "Hello," she said guardedly. "Who are you?"

Violet unconsciously gripped the lapels of her cotton robe together. The garment was modestly cut and thick enough to hide her shape, but something about the redhead made her feel terribly exposed.

"Hello," she replied in a raspy voice, then deliberately cleared her throat before going on. "I'm Violet."

The redhead removed her dark glasses as she climbed the wooden steps. "I'm Justine Pardee. Charlie's mother. Is my son here?"

This was Charlie's mother? She couldn't be old enough! Dumbfounded, Violet slowly nodded. "Yes. But he's still asleep."

"Oh." Justine eased down in the chair next to Violet. "I heard last night that he'd come home, and I couldn't wait any longer to see him," she explained, then smiled warmly. "I didn't realize he'd brought company with him."

Violet's cheeks blushed deep red. Dear Heaven, what must his mother be thinking? Whatever it was, it couldn't be good.

"Oh, I'm not company," she said quickly, then thinking that probably sounded peculiar she added, "I mean, Charlie just picked me up on the highway."

Justine Pardee's brows winged upward, and Violet could see her response had only made the situation seem even worse.

"You see, it's my car. It broke down, and Charlie was kind enough to stop and help me."

Understanding suddenly dawned in the other woman's eyes, and she nodded at Violet. "That would be my son. He still thinks he's the Durango Kid."

Violet's brow puckered. "I beg your pardon?"

Justine chuckled softly. "I'm sorry. Unless you're an old movie fan, you're far too young to know who the Kid was. He was a Saturday-afternoon matinee idol. A cowboy version of Sir Galahad."

So it wasn't unusual for Charlie to go around saving damsels in distress. Violet was probably just one of many. No more special than the first or the last one.

"Well, I tried to assure him I could manage on my own, but somehow I ended up out here," Violet tried to explain. The last thing she wanted was to have this lovely woman thinking she'd tried to seduce her son in any way.

Suddenly there was a shuffle of feet at the door. Both

women looked around to see Sam's little face pressed against the screen.

"I'm hungry, Mommy. When are we gonna eat?"

Violet glanced at Justine. Her eyes were shining with a smile as she observed Sam just inside the door.

"This is your son?"

Violet nodded, then motioned for Sam to come to her. The boy trotted barefoot across the porch and sidled up to his mother's knee.

"Mrs. Pardee, this is my son, Sam."

"Hello, Sam," Justine said gently. "How old are you?"

"Four," he announced, holding up the fingers to match.

"Only four! My goodness you look big enough to be five or six!" she exclaimed.

Sam giggled. "I'm nearly five and I like to eat. Mommy says that makes me grow."

"You know what? Charlie likes to eat, too," Justine told him. "So why don't we go to the kitchen and find something for breakfast?"

"Yeah! I like pancakes!"

"Sam! You little beggar, you'll eat what's in the kitchen!" Violet exclaimed. Her son had never been the bashful sort. But she'd never seen him take to anyone as quickly as he had Charlie and now his mother.

"Oh, don't scold him for being honest," Justine said to Violet with a tinkling laugh, then taking Sam by the hand, she led him toward the door. "Come on, Sam. If the ants haven't found the syrup, we'll have pancakes. And if Charlie doesn't wake up by the time they're cooked, we'll eat his, too."

Inside the house Violet slowly followed the two of them to the kitchen. Along the way she glanced over her shoulder to see Charlie's bedroom door was still shut. With all the noise that was going on now, she doubted he could still be asleep, and she wondered what he'd think about finding his mother here so early.

In the kitchen Justine went to the refrigerator and pulled open the door. Empty shelves stared back at her. "My son didn't bring any fresh groceries with him?"

"He did. But they're still in the ice chest. The refrigerator was shut off. He was waiting for it to cool down."

"Roy and I decided to unplug it. Our son gets home so rarely these days the whole inside would mold over between visits."

The woman's remark surprised Violet. She'd sensed that Charlie was fond, even proud, of this place. And Texas wasn't all that far from here. Did he stay away because he had to or because the need to come back home rarely hit him?

"When—uh, was the last time Charlie was here?" Violet asked her.

With a grimace Justine shut the door and crossed to the cabinets where she pulled a white apron from one of the drawers and tied it around her slender waist. "About a year ago. Of course it hasn't been that long since I've seen him. Roy and I travel to Fort Worth from time to time." Glancing at Violet she asked, "Where are you from? I hear the South in your voice."

"Georgia, originally. Texas the past few years."

"I've never been as far east as Georgia. But I've been to Mississippi. We rode down the river on a steamboat. I'll never forget it. All that history and beauty."

Amazed at the woman's open friendliness, she could do little more than nod.

Justine opened the cabinets and pulled down a plastic canister of flour. "Actually, there's a lot of history and beauty around here, too," she went on. "And not unlike the South, there was a war fought here, too. First between the settlers and the Apaches. Then came the Lincoln County range war.''

''I've heard of it,'' Violet replied. ''Movies have been made about the fierce gun battles between the ranchers. But I didn't realize the range war was in this area.''

Justine opened another cabinet door in search of a bowl. ''On this very ground,'' Justine told her. ''You're in Lincoln County.''

Violet settled Sam in a chair at the table, then joined Charlie's mother at the counter. Just being in the same room with the woman made her feel disheveled and awkward and totally out of place.

''Is there something I can do?''

With sudden misgivings, Justine glanced at Violet. ''Oh, I'm sorry, Violet. I guess it looks like I've just barged in and taken over.''

''It doesn't—'' she cleared her throat ''—please, don't apologize. It's your place to take over. I'm—just here because of—circumstance.''

Justine waved away her words with a wooden spoon. ''It doesn't matter why you're here, honey. I'm sure Charlie wants you to feel at home, and I do, too. So dig out some bacon or sausage or whatever the Kid brought to eat, and we'll have breakfast.''

Violet couldn't believe Charlie's mother was being so warm and accepting to a woman she'd only met minutes before. She'd never had a mother-in-law. Brent's mother had passed away when he'd been a young child, and Rex had never remarried.

She knew most of the bad mother-in-law stories she heard were wildly exaggerated. Still, she figured the woman who got Justine for a mother-in-law would be lucky indeed.

While Justine mixed the pancake batter, Violet put on a skilletful of bacon and sausage to fry. Once it was sizzling, she poured Sam a glass of orange juice and sent him out on the porch to drink it.

She was placing plates around the farm table when Charlie walked into the kitchen. His only attempt at modesty was a pair of faded blue jeans, and as Violet's gaze dipped downward over his bare chest, she knew she'd never seen such raw sensuality in her whole life. He looked like a man who pumped iron, but Violet seriously doubted his job allowed him any time for the gym. More than likely he got all those muscles from lifting women into his arms.

Sandy hair flopped into his sleepy eyes. He raked it back with a rough hand, then skimmed a glance over Violet before turning his attention to Justine, who was yet unaware her son had entered the room.

Without a word he walked up behind her and slipped his arms around her waist. "Hi, Mom."

"Charlie!"

She whirled around and smacked kisses on both sides of his face. "Look at you! You look like death warmed over! You're so skinny!"

She poked her fingers at his washboard abdomen, causing a half grin to curve his lips. And Violet suddenly had her answer. For all his gruffness and sarcasm, Charlie was glad to see his mother.

"I weigh over two hundred pounds, Mom. I can't be skinny."

"Well, you look as gaunt as a racehorse to me," she protested, then sniffed as tears welled up in her eyes.

Charlie glanced at Violet as if to say *I told you so.* Violet was amazed to find a lump had collected in her own throat. To think Charlie had once been this woman's little boy, just as Sam was hers now, touched a spot in Violet.

"It looks like you two have already introduced yourselves," he said to his mother.

"Yes, we did. And I can't believe you were lying in bed instead of keeping this beautiful young woman company."

His sidelong glance at Violet was mocking. "Violet doesn't need my company," he drawled. "She just needs her car fixed."

Moving down the counter, he poured himself a cup of coffee from the drip machine Violet had used earlier this morning. After a couple of careful sips, he asked his mother, "How did you know I was here?"

"Randall spilled the beans," she said as she flipped two perfectly browned pancakes.

"I should have known. You'd have to put duct tape on that guy's mouth to keep him quiet," he muttered irritably. "I don't know how Dad has put up with him all these years."

Justine's head twisted around, and she stared at her son with dismay. "Charlie! That's an awful thing to say. Randall has been more than a working colleague with your father all these years. He's also been his friend. Why, if it wasn't for Randall, Roy might not have ever learned you were his son."

Charlie rolled his eyes. "That's exactly what I'm talking about. The man can't keep his mouth shut."

From Justine's expression, Violet could tell the woman was disappointed, even disturbed by Charlie's attitude. Since she didn't know the person they were talking about, it was impossible to know who was in the right. Yet the whole thing told Violet that Charlie was obviously acting out of character and it was troubling his mother.

"I thought you always liked Randall," Justine said. She lifted the pancakes from the skillet and placed them on the stack she'd already cooked.

"I do like the man," Charlie conceded. "He just needs to keep his mouth shut."

Justine sighed but didn't say anything else. Charlie

glanced around the room, then settled his gaze on Violet. "Where's Sam? Still asleep?"

She was surprised he'd noticed the absence of her son. Though he'd been kind to Sam, he hadn't gone out of his way to pay attention to him, either.

"He's drinking his orange juice on the front porch," she told him, then deciding now would be a good time to give Charlie and his mother a few moments alone, she added, "The pancakes are almost ready. I'll go get him."

Once she had scurried out of the room, Charlie moved back over to the gas range where his mother was pouring the last of the batter into a black iron skillet.

"Did Violet explain why she was here?" he asked.

"Her car. You've already said as much," Justine answered, then glanced over her shoulder at him. "Why? Is there something else?"

Grimacing, Charlie shrugged. "Money."

When she didn't make any response, he said, "Aren't you going to groan and tell me I'm a fool?"

His mother gave him a wry smile, and Charlie suddenly realized how much he'd missed his family and how long it had been since he'd been able to spend time and be a real part of them.

"No. You're a grown man. You ought to know what you're doing by now."

He ought to, Charlie thought. But he didn't. Where women were concerned he'd started out on a bad course and headed downward ever since. It wasn't that he didn't like female companionship. Truth was he probably liked it too much. But women needed time and attention. They needed a man to commit their heart and soul to them. They couldn't understand that the star pinned to his breast was the real love of his life.

"I'm not like Dad," he said.

"What is that supposed to mean?"

"He has you."

"Oh, Charlie, you—" she began gently, then broke off as Violet and Sam entered the room.

Violet glanced from mother to son and back again. "Is— would you like for us to wait outside a few more minutes?"

Charlie and Justine stared at her, and Violet's face blushed deep pink. "Well, uh—I know you two haven't seen each other in a while and you'd probably like to talk alone."

Justine was the first to respond. "Don't be silly, Violet. The pancakes are all ready. Charlie and I don't need to be alone to talk. Do we, son?"

"No. Mother's good at talking even in a crowd. She's never at a loss for words."

Chuckling, Justine went to the gas range and collected the plate of pancakes. "I imagine Violet has already figured out for herself that I'm a little gabby."

Sam tugged on his mother's hand. "Mommy, what's gabby? Does that mean she's sick?"

Justine laughed while Violet shook her head at her son. "No. That means she talks a lot. Like you do sometimes."

Justine placed the pancakes and meat platter in the middle of the table and everyone took their seats and began to fill their plates.

In spite of his slender build Sam was a hearty eater. He paid little attention to the adults as he stuffed bites of syrup-drenched pancakes into his mouth.

Still feeling as if she was in the way, Violet concentrated on her food, too. She didn't want Justine or Charlie to feel as though they had to include her in their conversation. She was a stranger to them. They were family. And not the sort of family she'd come from. She could tell just by the interaction between mother and son that the Pardees were a loving, closely knit group.

"How is Caroline?" Charlie eventually asked. "Is she going to be coming home anytime soon?"

"Your sister is fine. But I doubt she'll be coming home while you're here. She's going to be showing some of her jewelry in California for the next few weeks."

Charlie reached for the platter of meat, and as he helped himself to several slices of bacon, Violet wondered what his life back in Fort Worth was like. Did he cook for himself or eat out? Did a girlfriend or live-in love see that he was fed in the morning or after a hard day's work? She knew it was crazy, even dangerous to be so curious about him. But she couldn't seem to stop herself. It was like he'd already become rooted in her brain and she couldn't pull him out.

"I guess Dad had already gone to work when you headed over here," he said to his mother.

Justine shook her head. "Actually he was coming with me, but before we could get into the truck he got a call. He said to tell you he'd see you later."

He reached for his coffee cup. "Duty calls."

Violet glanced at Justine. Did the older woman detect the acidity in her son's voice, or had Violet imagined it?

"Oh, yes, duty calls," she said between bites. "After all these years of being a sheriff's son and then being a lawman yourself, you know all about it." She glanced across the table at Violet. "I noticed you aren't wearing a wedding band. Have you ever been married?"

"Mom!" Charlie growled.

"Oh, hush, Charlie," she scolded cheerfully. "I'm sure you've already asked."

Once again Violet felt herself blushing. She wasn't used to being the topic of discussion. While growing up she'd been a bone of contention between her parents, so she had deliberately avoided joining their conversations. She wouldn't know what it was like to be as Charlie, with two loving parents making a fuss over her.

"My husband was killed in a plane crash a little over a year ago," she said to Justine.

Justine's expression was suddenly full of compassion. "Oh, my dear, how awful for you. I was just going to tell you that at times being married to a lawman is almost being like a widow. But you obviously know how wrong that is. *Almost* isn't anything like what you're going through."

Violet's eyes darted from Justine to Charlie. His attention was on his plate, his features closed. He wasn't married, and he was a lawman. Was there a connection? she wondered. Or had Charlie simply had a bad experience with a woman?

"I wouldn't know anything about lawmen or their married life," Violet told her. "But I do know about being a widow."

Justine shook her head regretfully. "I'm sorry you had to learn at such an early age. It isn't fair. But then Charlie will tell you the only fair he knows about has show animals and carnival rides."

The sidelong glance he shot at his mother was mocking. "A person is better off knowing the odds are against him from the start, Mom. A man with stars in his eyes is only bound to get hurt."

Justine studied her son for a moment, and Violet knew there was something on her mind she wanted to tell him, but the other woman merely sighed and went back to eating her breakfast. Violet did the same.

Nearly an hour later, after breakfast was eaten and the kitchen clean again, Justine announced she had to get back to the ranch. Charlie immediately grabbed her by the arm and insisted on walking her out to her pickup.

Once mother and son reached the vehicle, Justine smiled

slyly up at him. "Okay. What do you want to say to me that you couldn't in front of Violet?"

Charlie shook his head with resignation. "I can't ever fool you, can I?"

Justine laughed. "Not much," she said, then her laughter sobered and she asked, "Are you worried you're going to be stuck with this woman or worried that you're not?"

The rush of air that passed his lips was something between a laugh and a rough sigh. "I don't know. What do you think...about her, I mean?"

Her eyes scanned his strong face. "What I think doesn't matter. It's what you think."

Charlie thought Violet meant trouble for him. But if he were to tell his mother that, she wouldn't understand. On the other hand she might understand too much. That was the problem with being close to someone, he thought. They could read him, see inside him and know what his heart was really feeling. He wasn't about to let Violet get that close.

"Like I told you earlier, she has a money problem. She doesn't have enough to get her car repaired. She needs a job."

"What sort of skills does she have?"

He glanced back at the house. Violet and Sam were on the porch, but they were too far away to hear any of his conversation. "She said she'd been working as a bookkeeper. But you and I both know that no employer would bother hiring someone for a job of that sort unless they intended to stay for the long haul. And Violet insists she's heading on to California."

"California?" Justine repeated quizzically. "What's there? Some of her family?"

Charlie shook his head. "She doesn't have family. There's nothing in California for her except this dream she has of making a home for her and her son there."

Justine considered his words. "There's nothing wrong with that. A woman has a right to dream, Charlie, even if she can't make it come true in the next year or even the next."

"Oh hell, Mom, I understand that. But Violet doesn't need to be—well, it doesn't make sense—it's not safe or practical for her to be driving her and her son off to God only knows where without someone to watch out for them."

Justine sighed. "Is that what this is all about, Charlie, her safety? Son, I know you need to—"

Charlie quickly interrupted with a shake of his head. The last thing he wanted was a lecture from his mother. She normally kept her opinions to herself, but on those rare occasions she did let loose on him, Charlie usually ended up feeling like hell. Mainly because she was always right, and he was too stubborn to admit it. "I know that's none of my business. I just think...I'm going to offer her a job and a place to stay here. Until she can get her car fixed."

If Justine was surprised at his plans, she didn't show it. Instead, she patted his big hand which was still wrapped around her forearm. "I don't see anything wrong with that, son. But what sort of job are you talking about?"

He shrugged. "Well, the place has been needing some work done on it for some time. I thought Violet might help me do some painting and wallpapering. Things like that. I realize it wouldn't be like bookkeeping, but at least it would be a job."

Justine nodded thoughtfully. "Now that you mention it, I might have a little work for Violet, too. Since your cousin Emily gave birth to little Harlan Cooper, she's been doing accounting work again in her home, so your dad and I turned our ranch books over to her. But I still have a lot of personal record keeping that she could do for me."

"Would you really be willing to do that?" Charlie asked.

Smiling gently, she said, "I like your Violet. If I can help her, I'll be glad to."

Charlie shot her a wearied but indulgent look. "She's not *my* Violet, Mom. And don't even begin to think it."

Justine chuckled. "I know, darling. You've sworn off women. How could I forget?"

He frowned at her, and she raised up on tiptoe and kissed his cheek. "I've got to go. When you get rested and caught up around here, bring Violet over to the ranch and I'll box up all the paperwork I've been neglecting. And if you decide to come around suppertime we might just be having chili *rellenos,*" she added impishly.

Charlie opened the door for her, then stepped back after she'd climbed in and started the motor.

"We'll be over soon," he promised, then lifted his hand in farewell.

After his mother's truck had disappeared behind the desert hills, Charlie turned and walked slowly back to the house. Violet was sitting on the floor of the porch with Sam, looking almost like a teenager as she pushed a little tractor back and forth to her son.

Since breakfast, she had dressed in a pair of yellow shorts and a turquoise blouse. Her hair was pulled into a ponytail on the crown of her head. Yet her sad, wary eyes gave her away. She wasn't a carefree teenager. She was a widow with problems.

Violet glanced up at Charlie as he climbed the steps. "Is everything all right?"

"Yes. Why? What could be wrong?"

She ignored Sam's persistent pat on her leg and continued to look up at Charlie. "Me, I suppose."

Charlie gave her one of his rare, twisted grins. "I really didn't see my mother giving you the cold shoulder."

"No. Your mother couldn't have been nicer. But she

loves you. I expect she would treat anyone in your house with respect."

"Not anyone," he disagreed. "She's not *that* nice."

He walked across the porch and took a seat in one of the wooden chairs.

"Mommy, you're not playing anymore," Sam reminded her. "Can I go get my other toys?"

Violet turned her attention to her son. "Yes. But only the ones in the green bag. Don't get into our suitcases And after you find the toys, come right back here to the porch."

"Okay," he promised, then raced into the house.

The screen door banged loudly behind him. Violet sighed. "I'm sorry about all this."

"This?" he asked dryly.

Nodding, she glanced away from him. "This noise. This trouble. This interruption of your vacation."

Charlie couldn't recall knowing anyone who apologized as much as Violet. She seemed to truly feel she was a burden. Was this an idea she always carried around with her, he wondered. Or was he causing her to feel unwanted and in the way?

"Can't you say something else besides I'm sorry?" he growled. "I'm the one who brought you here. If you're making me miserable, it's my own fault. Not yours."

Her nostrils flared as she turned her head slightly and stared at him. "You have such a wonderful way with words, Charlie Pardee," she drawled. "Now if you don't mind, I'd appreciate a ride into Ruidoso. Just name your price for the trip. I have the cash to pay you."

He pointed his finger at her. "That's another thing. You ought to know better than to tell someone you have cash on you."

Violet couldn't stop herself. She leaned across the space separating them, grabbed his forefinger and wrenched it backward. "Don't be pointing at me," she said hotly. "I asked you for a ride. Not a safety lecture!"

She dropped his hand and he glared at her as he rubbed the middle knuckle. "Where did you get that temper? It's going to get you into trouble," he warned.

"Funny, but till I met you I didn't know I had one," she quipped.

"I'll bet."

She continued to hold his gaze. But it was very hard. Every time she looked into his azure blue eyes, all she could think about was the way he'd kissed her. The way his lips had felt and tasted, the way his big arms had crushed her up against his chest.

"What about the ride? Sam and I need to be on our way."

"Why the sudden rush?" he demanded. "You didn't appear to be in a hurry to leave here before breakfast."

She couldn't take it any longer. Her heart was thrumming, and her thoughts drifting. She had to look down and away from his eyes before she forgot what the heck they were talking about.

"I do have manners. And I didn't want to appear ungrateful. Especially in front of someone as gracious as your mother."

Folding his arms against his chest, Charlie stared out at the distant mesa. "I see. You don't want to insult my mother, but I'm a different matter."

She rubbed at a tiny freckle on the top of her thigh. "Not exactly. I don't necessarily want to insult you, either. I just want to get out of here."

Why were all women so independent nowadays? Charlie inwardly fumed. They all believed they knew how to take care of themselves and conquer the world in the process. And they didn't need a man to hold their hand while they did it. At least they didn't think they needed a man. He had altogether different ideas about that.

It was one of the reasons Charlie had quit looking for love. He was a man. And being needed was essential to the male makeup. It was as necessary as being loved. But so far Charlie hadn't found a woman who wanted him more than her independence, and he hadn't found a woman he wanted more than being a ranger.

Dropping his hold on her wrist, he gave her a smirk that vaguely resembled a smile. "Forget about going into Ruidoso. You're staying here for a while."

She sucked in a shocked breath. "Staying here? Says who?"

"Me. I'm offering you a job. No—I'm offering you two jobs."

Charlie's words brought Violet rushing to her feet. With her hands jammed in her shorts pockets, she circled around to the front of Charlie's chair and stared at him as if he were a fresh discovery under a microscope.

"You're offering me a job? What do you mean? What sort of job?"

His blue eyes sliced across her face. "Hmm. Now you're interested. A few minutes ago you wanted to get the hell out of here. But that shouldn't surprise me. Every woman I've ever met is fickle."

Hating to be grouped with the women he'd known in the past, she said, "You imply you know all about women, but I'm wondering how that's possible when you've never been married."

His expression turned cagey. "You don't have to marry a woman to know what she's all about," he assured her.

"Really? I guess you think 'playing house' is just as...enlightening as marriage."

Charlie had never "played house" with any woman. He'd come close once with Angela. Over several months his feelings for the tall blonde had grown from mild interest to what he'd believed was love. It had been a slow, gradual thing, careful and well thought out on his part. He'd truly wanted her to be his wife and he'd thought she had wanted the same thing. But when he'd finally proposed, she'd simply laughed at him. Did he honestly think any woman would be fool enough to marry him? she'd asked. He could barely unpin the badge from his shirt long enough to have dinner, much less be a husband.

The confrontation over his desire to marry had ended their relationship. Charlie had never been so hurt and humiliated in his life, but the experience had well and truly opened his eyes about women and his job. Since Angela, he'd kept his enjoyment of females on a casual basis. And even those times had grown scarce in the past year.

"I've been—enlightened enough to know I don't want a wife." He stood up and gazed down at her with hard eyes and a grim mouth. "Now what about the jobs? Do you want them or not?"

The closer the man was to her, the weaker she got, Violet decided. As she tilted her head back to look at him, every nerve in her body stretched as taut as a guitar string.

"You haven't told me what they are."

"Painting, cleaning, hanging wallpaper, things like that."

"Where?"

"Here. For me."

She tried not to look as shocked as she felt. "What's the other job?"

"My mother has some bookkeeping she'd like you to do for her."

So he'd discussed her situation with his mother. She didn't know whether to be furious, flattered or just downright grateful.

She glanced away from him and swallowed as a ball of

mixed emotions knotted her throat. "I don't know what to say. I never expected anything like this." She looked back at him. "What would I be paid?"

"The repair bill on your car."

"The mechanic said it would take a few hundred." She couldn't believe Charlie or his mother had that much work for her to do.

"I remember what the mechanic said."

If he wasn't such a rock-hard wall of muscle she would have tried to shake him. "I don't want pity, Charlie. Or handouts. I think it would be better if you took us into Ruidoso so I could hunt for a legitimate job."

It probably would be better for all of them, Charlie silently agreed. But it was too late for that. While traveling through the desert he'd found a little sage hen with a broken wing. He couldn't allow her to try to fly again until he fixed her.

"What's the matter? Scared of getting your hands dirty?"

Her spine stiffened and her lips pursed to a thin, angry line. "No. I don't think I'm too good for manual labor. But—"

"Good. We'll start after you get unpacked."

He turned to go as if to end the discussion then and there. Violet grabbed him by the forearm. He glanced back at her, and she swallowed as her heart beat heavy with anticipation. "Sam and I are going to continue to stay here with you?"

"Where else?"

Violet could think of a thousand, a million other places she should be rather than here with this Texas Ranger. Yet she couldn't think of one where she wanted to be more. And that was the most terrifying part of all.

"All right. I guess I'll take the jobs."

Nodding, he started to move away, yet once again Violet

tightened her hold on his arm. His questioning gaze lifted from her small fingers wrapped around his flesh up to her face.

"Thank you, Charlie."

He started to tell her she might not be thanking him after everything was said and done. But something on her face touched him, pierced the hard crust around his heart.

"You're welcome, Violet," he murmured huskily, then turned and left her on the porch, staring after him.

Chapter Five

Violet had just cleaned the remnants of lunch from the kitchen table when Charlie's father, Roy, pulled up in a pickup with a stock trailer hitched to the back.

Sam immediately came running in from the front yard, squealing that a man had come with horses. Charlie went out to greet him, and in spite of Violet's attempts to keep him inside, Sam followed right on his heels.

Choosing to stay inside, Violet walked over to a living room window and watched her son trot out to where the two men were standing near the stock trailer.

Meeting Justine had been one thing, she thought, but the sheriff of Lincoln County was another matter entirely. For all she knew Rex might have asked the Amarillo police to put out a missing person bulletin on her and Sam. If so, Roy Pardee might have seen it, taken one look at her, and concluded she was Violet O'Dell. It was a long shot, but lawmen, especially one who had been in the business as long as Charlie's father, had unusually keen eyes.

But would Rex actually go so far as to contact the police?

she wondered for the thousandth time. Her father-in-law had sworn he would if she ever left with his grandson. And he was a man who always made good on his threats. The men who worked for him could attest to that. Still, if the truth behind his business ever came out, Rex stood the chance of losing a lot more than his grandson. Violet only wished she could be the one to expose him.

From her view at the window, Violet watched the men unload the horses. A big gray and a smaller sorrel. Once they were safely out of the trailer, Charlie led them over to a barn a few yards north of the house. Roy followed, and Sam tagged along at the older man's side.

As the sheriff sauntered over the dusty ground, Violet could see where Charlie had gotten his fine looks. The older man was not as tall or heavily built as his son, but even though he had to be in his late fifties, he was still a very fit, handsome man.

Charlie looped the reins of both horses over a hitching post, and the two men ambled over to the nearest shed. They talked for several minutes, and Violet had decided to go back to her work of cleaning the kitchen cabinets when she noticed the sheriff turn his attention to Sam.

Squatting down on his heels, it appeared as if he asked Sam a question because the boy immediately began to bob his head up and down. Then before she could guess what it was all about, Charlie reached down and plucked her son off his feet.

When he carried him over to the big gray and sat him astride the animal, she gasped. Sam had never been on a horse before! This one was huge and wasn't even wearing a saddle!

Instantly forgetting her plan to stay out of sight, Violet ran out of the house. By the time she reached the barn, Charlie was leading the horse in a small circle in front of the barn. Sam's grin said he was in heaven.

"Hi, Mommy! Look at me! I'm riding a horse. See how big he is?"

Curbing the urge to snatch him off the animal, Violet stopped just short of their circular path.

"Yes...I see how big he is. But don't you think you've had enough riding for now?"

"No! I want to take a long ride with Charlie. He said we could ride way out in the hills and look for cows and coyotes."

Violet didn't know what shocked her the most. Charlie's suggestion of spending time with her son, or how eager Sam was to go with him. In either case, she was terrified of him falling and breaking bones or being trampled.

Even though Sam had been born and raised in Texas, and his father and grandfather had been in the packing plant business, he hadn't lived on a ranch or been around livestock. The few times Sam visited his father's work place, he'd seen the horses and feedlots full of cattle at a distance. But that was all. Brent had never wanted his son to grow up being a cowboy. There were already too damn many of them in Texas, he'd always said. Violet had often wanted to remind him that without the cowboys he wouldn't have a business at all.

Steps sounded beside her. She glanced around to see Charlie's father walking up to her, and her heart jolted with sudden fear.

"There's really nothing to worry about ma'am. Ole Joe is as gentle as a dog, and Charlie's not going to let him fall off."

Violet knew she probably looked wild-eyed and hysterical. But for the past few months she'd had nothing but worries and fears. Especially the fear of losing her son.

Swallowing nervously, she did her best to nod at Charlie's father. "I'm sure you're right. I'm just a little...nervous. You see, Sam's never been on a horse before.''

"I figured as much when I asked him about riding." He thrust his hand toward Violet. "I'm Charlie's father, Roy."

Even though he was the sheriff, shaking hands with Roy wasn't nearly as disconcerting as when Charlie had wrapped his big fingers around hers.

"I'm Violet. Your son—"

With a knowing smile he held up his hand. "You don't have to explain anything to me. I'm just glad you're here."

Glad? With the man being a lawman, Violet would have figured he would be suspicious of any strange woman settling into his son's vacation home.

"You don't want to know why I'm here?"

Roy Pardee chuckled, and Violet decided if Charlie possessed just an ounce of his father's laid-back charm, he'd be nigh impossible to resist.

"If you can keep Charlie's mind off his job, I don't care why you're here."

Violet was about to ask the man what he meant by that when Charlie led the horse and Sam over to them.

"Well, Sam, it looks like your mama is chomping at the bit to get you off Joe," Charlie said to the boy.

He lifted Sam from the horse's back and set him down in front of Violet. She was relieved her son didn't whine or cry in protest. But in the past twenty-four hours, she'd noticed that Charlie seemed to bring out the little man in her son. She could only suppose that Sam was either eager to have Charlie's admiration or he was scared the Ranger would scold him for misbehaving.

"Can I ride later, Charlie?" Sam asked. "Are you still gonna look for cows and coyotes?"

He nodded at the child, then glanced at Violet. Her white face angered him. The woman worried about everything she shouldn't, rather than the things she should.

''We might even look for sidewinders, Sam.''

Violet glared at him through narrowed eyes. ''Come on,'' she said to Sam. ''It's time you came back to the house with me.''

As the two men watched her go, Roy's expression turned to one of wry speculation. ''I believe you ruffled her feathers a bit.''

Charlie grunted. ''I meant to ruffle her. She's going to make a mama's boy out of Sam, and I hate to see it.''

Roy glanced at his son. ''Justine told me Violet had recently been widowed. I expect that would make any woman a little overprotective.''

''I'm sure it would. A little. But not to the point of obsession. Mom never treated me that way and you know it. If she had, I would have grown up a sissy.''

''Your mother never had to deal with the death of her husband,'' he pointed out, then, adjusting the brim of his hat on his forehead, he added, ''Charlie, sometimes you expect too much out of people. Especially yourself.''

''What's that suppose to mean?'' Charlie asked sharply.

Roy's brief smile was that of an indulgent parent. ''Once you figure it out, son, you won't have the problem anymore,'' he said, then slapped him affectionately on the shoulder. ''Enjoy the horses. I've got to get home and pack a bag. Randall and I have to head to Las Cruces in the morning, and I'm afraid we're going to have to stay over a day or two.''

''Thanks for bringing them over to me, Dad. And be careful on your trip.''

As he turned to go, Roy tapped the badge pinned to his breast and grinned. ''Careful is my middle name, son.''

Charlie waved, but he didn't grin back.

Violet pumped the trigger on the spray gun. Liquid cleanser blasted the cabinet door then slid in brown rivulets to the countertop. As she swiped a cloth back and forth over the gooey, grimy wood, she wondered again how she had gotten from her home in Amarillo to here. True, the house she'd lived in with her father-in-law had not been a real home to her. But she hadn't left it to go to work for a Texas Ranger. An arrogant, know-it-all one at that!

She was scrubbing the wood viciously when a quiet voice shattered the silence.

"Picturing that cabinet door as my face?"

From her precarious perch on the countertop, Violet jerked around to see Charlie had slipped into the kitchen and right up behind her. She hadn't known he was anywhere around, and the sight of him nearly made her lose her balance.

"Among other things," she muttered. "I thought you'd be long gone by now. Out on the range hunting rattlesnakes."

His expression unmoving, he said, "I will be. When the sun gets a little lower. Besides, I'm not going without Sam. Not after I promised him."

Gripping the edge of the counter, she twisted around far enough to be facing him head on. "Over my dead body!"

Laughter erupted from him. "Violet, if I really wanted to take Sam on a horseback ride, I wouldn't have to kill you to do it!"

His words were a mimicry to all the threats she'd heard in the past months. And suddenly without warning it was Rex's voice in her head, not Charlie's. *It wouldn't be hard for me to get custody of Sam. All I would have to do is bring up your brush with the law back in Georgia, and you'd never see your son again!*

Rage at Charlie, at Rex, at men in general began to boil her blood. Before she knew what she was about to do, she jumped down from the cabinet counter, flung herself straight at him and pummeled his broad chest with both fists.

"You bully! You hateful—man! Don't you threaten me! Ever!"

Charlie had expected his words to rile her a little. He supposed he'd even wanted them to. She irritated the hell out of him in a thousand ways, and he wanted to get back at her somehow. But in his wildest imaginings he hadn't expected her to flog him.

"Damn it, Violet! Calm down!" Charlie finally managed to snatch both her wrists. He held her firmly until she finally stopped fighting and sagged weakly against him.

"What in the heck was that all about?" he demanded. "Have you gone crazy?"

Violet knew her face was red from exertion and embarrassment, and she could see Charlie's eyes watching her breast heave to regain her breath. Without a doubt she'd acted like a wild woman and still looked like one. But for once she didn't care. When she'd left Amarillo, she'd made a promise to herself never to let another man try to control her. And she'd be damned before she did!

"I was crazy for ever agreeing to stay here with you," she said angrily. "This time I'm leaving. And I mean it!"

Any other time Charlie would have been furious with her. But curiosity over her fierce reaction erased any anger he was feeling.

"We've already been over all this," he said curtly. "And I don't understand why you've gone so wild all of a sudden."

As Violet looked up at him, it dawned on her that he couldn't possibly know why she was so angry and so desperate to get away. And above all else, she mustn't let him find out.

Her eyes fell from his and her shoulders slumped. "Sam

is my son. Not yours. I won't let you take him over...just because...you're doing me a favor.''

His expression was incredulous. ''I have no intention of taking over your son!''

She looked at him with disbelief. ''No? You put him on that horse without even asking my permission.''

He groaned, but Violet couldn't help thinking it sounded more like a growl. ''My word, Violet, I wouldn't put him or any child in danger!''

''A horse could kill him!''

He dropped her wrists and grabbed her by the shoulders. If his fingers were biting into her flesh, Violet didn't notice. She was gripped by his blue stare.

''A drive into Ruidoso could kill him!'' Charlie flung at her. ''Can't you see you need to ease off the reins a bit? You're going to make a sissy out of him!''

''My son is not a sissy! And anyway...it's none of your business.''

That was true, Charlie thought. But something about Sam made him remember back to when he was four years old and it had been just him and his mother. He'd been desperate to have a father show him how to do big-boy things. When his parents had eventually married, having his daddy around and spending time with him had been heaven. Charlie couldn't give Sam his own father back, but while they were here at the cabin, he could at least see the boy had a chance to experience the outdoors.

''No,'' he said coldly. ''I guess Sam isn't any of my business. I guess you aren't, either.''

He dropped his hold on her shoulders, and before Violet could guess his intentions, he walked out of the kitchen, then out of the house.

His leaving stunned her just as much as the things he'd said to her, and she looked around the small kitchen while still feeling his presence, the clamp of his strong fingers on her wrists and shoulders.

What was the man all about? she wondered. And why did she care if he was angry or disappointed with her? He was the one who'd gotten out of line!

You're making your son a sissy!

She'd wanted to slap his jaw when he'd flung the accusation at her. But now as she stood in the silent kitchen, the words haunted her. Was Charlie right? Had she, in her fear of losing him, been holding on to Sam too tightly?

Groaning aloud, she thrust dark hair off her moist forehead and walked over to the screen door leading out to the backyard. Sam was sitting under the sole cottonwood. Between his straddled legs was an assortment of trucks, tractors and farm animals, including horses. He had a vivid imagination and could entertain himself for hours if necessary. But she didn't want Sam to live only in his mind.

Slowly, she pushed through the screen door then walked down the steps and out to her son. The moment he spotted her, he looked up and grinned, and a pang of guilt rushed through Violet. Her son loved and needed her. Making his life happy and good was all she'd ever wanted.

"Hi, Mommy. Can you play with me now?"

She sat down beside him on the sandy ground. "I'm not finished with my work yet. Maybe I can play later. Right now, I want to talk to you about something."

Talking wasn't at all like playing. He turned his attention back to his toys, and Violet watched him carefully place a Hampshire hog in the back of a pickup truck, then push the truck over to an exposed root of the cottonwood.

"Okay," he mumbled, his thoughts already drifting to whatever fate he had planned for the hog.

"Did you like riding Charlie's horse?" Violet asked him.

The word *horse* did the trick. Sam looked at his mother with bright, attentive eyes. "Yeah! It was real fun!"

"You weren't afraid you were going to fall off?"

His little face wrinkled up as though he considered her question ridiculous. "No, Mommy. Charlie promised he wouldn't let me fall. And Charlie wouldn't lie."

He seemed so certain, so trusting of the man. And he'd only met him yesterday. Her son couldn't know that Charlie was a man who could ultimately hurt them both. And that was something she didn't want her son to know. She never wanted him to learn of the threats and dark clouds hanging over their heads. One of these days it would all be over. She had to hold on to that hope, otherwise she didn't know if she could go on.

"I see," she said thoughtfully. "So you believe Charlie's going to take care of you?"

Sam nodded emphatically. "Sure. He's a Texas Ranger. When he works, he wears a pistol and a badge. And sometimes he rides a horse after bad guys."

Apparently Sam had absorbed every word Charlie had said to him and been properly impressed, to boot. "I'm sure he does," Violet murmured, while picturing Charlie tracking down a thief, or even worse, a killer. Something about him told her he would be a relentless lawman. One who would never give up until he got his man. If he went after a woman with the same single-mindedness, Violet thought, she wouldn't have a chance.

"Do you still want to ride with him to hunt for cows?"

Sam jumped to his feet. "Yeah!"

Before Violet could say anything else, Sam was on his feet, racing to the house. "Where are you going?" she called after him.

"I gotta get my jeans on! Charlie says I can't ride with him unless I cover my legs and arms."

Violet watched her son scoot on into the house. Then she slowly rose to her feet and brushed off the seat of her shorts. She'd never seen Sam this excited over anything.

Not his birthday party, Christmas presents or a trip to the zoo or swimming pool. His eagerness made her wonder even more if she'd failed to see her son's need to be a little boy in the most basic sense.

She left the shade of the cottonwood and went into the house. She found Sam in the bedroom. Clothes were scattered all around the open suitcase lying atop the bed. She picked up two pair of shorts from the floor and tossed them onto the bed with the rest of the things.

"Sam, I'm not sure Charlie is ready to go yet," she told him, then smiled indulgently when he looked at her with great disappointment. "But once you get your clothes changed, you may go down to the barn and tell him I said it was okay for you to go riding. But don't get in the way or pester him. All right?"

Curbing the urge to caution him further, she left him to dress himself and went back to the kitchen to continue her cleaning job on the cabinets. After a few moments she heard the front door bang and knew Sam was on his way to the barn.

More than thirty minutes later she was standing at the sink, rinsing her cleaning cloth, when she saw Charlie leading the gray from under the loafing shed connected to the barn. Sam was already in the saddle, clinging to the big, flat horn. An old crumpled straw hat, several sizes too large was riding low on his little ears.

Violet hurried out to the front porch, then stood on the edge, one hand braced against a post. Sam saw her and waved excitedly. Charlie glanced briefly over his shoulder at her, then swung himself up in the saddle behind Sam.

Her heart sank as he reined the horse toward the north away from the house. He wasn't going to bother riding by the porch to assure her Sam would be safe, that she was right in letting her son go, or even to tell her a simple goodbye.

What was he, she asked herself, as she watched the horse and riders head toward the desert hills. A rock? A man without a heart or the ability to possess any sort of compassion or understanding where women were concerned?

The memory of Charlie hugging his mother flashed through her mind and she knew she could not doubt his love for Justine Pardee. It was the rest of the female population she had her doubts about.

"Mommy, we saw cows and a big windmill. It was going round and round in the wind, and it made water pour into a big tank so the cows and horses could drink. And we saw cactus called cho—choya. It had yellow flowers all over it, and I wanted to bring one home to you, but Charlie said if I did I'd get stickers in my hand and that would be painful."

Violet watched her son cram forkfuls of meat loaf into his mouth. "Sounds like you had a good time."

"It was lots of fun. And Joe is nice and really smart. Charlie doesn't even have to tell him where to go. He says that Joe's nose tells him where the cattle are, and he goes right to them."

"Is that so?" She glanced across the pine table at Charlie. He seemed to be concentrating entirely on his food and had said little more than five words since the three of them had sat down to supper. "What about coyotes? Did you see any of them?" she asked Sam.

"Naw," he answered. "Charlie says they're crafty and don't let humans see them too much."

Sounded like Charlie had said lots of things, Violet mused. Although it was hard for her to imagine. She got the impression it pained him to say anything to her unless it was something crass, a reprimand or a lecture.

Even though he hadn't acknowledged her gaze, Violet

continued to look at Charlie. "Uh—what about rattle-snakes, did you see any of those?"

"No," Sam said with great disappointment. "Charlie says they don't let people see them, either. He said I needed to watch and be careful not to get too close to one because when they bite you it can make you very sick and even die."

Sam was only four, nearing five years old. Too young to have to understand what the severity of "to die" meant. But he did. He knew his father had died when his plane had crashed to the earth, and he knew it meant Brent would never come back.

"Charlie is right," she told Sam.

This brought Charlie's head up, and his blue eyes looked straight into hers. She felt jolted at the contact.

"Can I go outside and play now, Mommy? I've ate all my food."

Violet forced herself to break his gaze and look at her son's plate. Seeing it was empty, she nodded her head at him. "Yes. But don't go any further than the tree in the backyard."

Sam scurried out of the room and left the two adults in strained silence. Violet finished her meat loaf and creamed spinach, then left the table to pour herself a cup of coffee.

She was standing at the cabinet counter, stirring cream into her coffee when he spoke, and her frayed nerves jerked at the unexpected sound.

"Sam is an obedient boy. He doesn't test the rules given to him."

"I'm glad you didn't have any problem with him," she said stiffly. "Are you ready for coffee?"

"Yes."

She poured him a cupful. As she placed it at his right elbow she couldn't stop her eyes from gliding over his thick, sandy brown hair, the wide width of his shoulders and the corded muscles of his forearms. He had everything a woman admired, except a heart.

"Thanks," he murmured.

With Sam out of the room, Violet couldn't bring herself to sit back down at the table with him, yet she didn't want to be so rude as to leave the room before he'd finished his meal.

Carrying her coffee cup with her, she ambled over to the screen door. Late-evening shadows were creeping across the barren yard. Sam was back in his spot beneath the cottonwood. No doubt hauling his Hampshire to a new farm.

"I don't think you understand what it's like to have a child," she said after a few moments.

He glanced over to where she was standing at the door. Her nose was against the screen, her expression wistful.

"Obviously I can't. I don't have one."

"You don't understand that he's all I have in this world."

Charlie's cup stopped halfway to his mouth as it struck him that she wasn't just a woman mouthing words or fishing for sympathy. And that made it all the more terrible.

"I recall you said you were adopted. But don't you have aunts or uncles or grandparents somewhere?"

The shortness was gone from his voice, and Violet decided to walk back over to the table. As she took the seat across from him, she said, "I have one uncle back in Georgia. But he…isn't much better than my father. I don't have anything to do with him."

Even though Charlie's grandparents were also gone, his family was still huge. If he were to ever need any sort of help they would come running. Violet was alone. Maybe he couldn't fathom the real meaning of that. Maybe no one could unless they were in her shoes.

"Did you ever try to get your father off alcohol?"

His question made her cringe inwardly. She'd done everything she could, not only to get her father off alcohol, but to try to make him see her as his daughter, to make him love her. Her efforts had not only failed, they'd gotten her into trouble. Trouble that was still looming over her head like an ominous thundercloud.

"I tried everything. I…well, I did the best I could to help him. But I never had much influence on my father. He didn't want an adopted child. He wanted one of his own. He went along with Mom's wishes to adopt me because she was ill and couldn't conceive. But later he made us both pay," she said bitterly.

"I can see why you might hate the man."

Hate him? Violet liked to believe she wasn't capable of hating anyone. But if it were possible, her hate would be directed at Rex, not Leroy. If given the chance, her father-in-law would try to take everything from her, whereas her father had only hurt her with his resentment and indifference.

Sighing, she jammed her hands into the pockets on her shorts. "No. I don't hate Leroy. I'm just wise enough to know that Sam and I are better off staying away from him. But none of that matters anymore, anyway. I simply wanted you to understand why I…get so protective of Sam sometimes. I wouldn't want to live without him."

It was plain that she loved her son, which was as it should be. But Charlie wasn't altogether sure the extent of her feelings was a good thing. She was a young woman. She should have wants or needs of her own, rather than just living for her son.

Charlie reached for a plate of cookies she'd set out for dessert. "Does Sam know he has a grandpa?"

Violet nodded. "Yes. The one in Amarillo. He's never seen my father, and it's very doubtful he ever will."

She said it with such gritty conviction that Charlie had to figure Violet's father was a pure bastard. She didn't seem the sort of woman who would turn her back on anyone, unless they had hurt her badly in some way.

As he had hurt her this afternoon, his thoughts tacked on. A part of Charlie felt bad about upsetting her. Yet he was still angry and perplexed because he didn't know exactly what he'd said or done to cause such an explosion in her. Maybe he'd been a little arrogant, but hell, all men were that way from time to time. He hadn't meant to hurt her.

"So this father-in-law back in Amarillo is basically the only family you have?"

Violet kept her eyes carefully on her coffee cup. "Yes."

Beneath a veil of dark brown lashes he studied her covertly. "Why didn't you want to stay there? Surely after all this time you acquired friends you enjoyed spending time with?"

His persistent questions not only annoyed her, they frightened her. She didn't want to think about her life back in Amarillo or what might happen if it ever caught up to her. She'd learned that Rex was a corrupt man. Legal or illegal, he would do anything to gain what he wanted. And he wanted total control of his grandson.

Lifting her head, she frowned at Charlie. "Can you ever stop being a Ranger? I'll bet you even wear that badge of yours to bed."

A surly grin twisted his lips. "Maybe I would if I had something to pin it to."

The meaning of his words hit her like a mouthful of hot chili peppers. Heat flooded her body and marked her face with color. "Why don't you try your chest? Your hide seems tough enough to handle it."

Before she knew what was happening, he was around the table, jerking her to her feet.

"What are you doing?" she gasped as he pulled her up against him.

"I'm going to show you something."

Violet's eyes widened at his menacing tone. "I don't—"

Her words stuck in her throat. Her heart hammered out of control as he tugged her hand up against his chest. "You really think I'm that hard?"

Everything about him was hard, Violet thought, even the stare of his cold blue eyes.

"You're...awful! Despicable!"

Her response brought a quirk of mocking humor to his face, and it was all Violet could do to keep from kicking his shin.

Without speaking one word, Charlie loosened a button on his shirt and slipped her hand inside. Violet's knees grew dangerously weak, and she closed her eyes as she fought to ignore the pleasure of his warm skin against her fingers.

"Does that feel tough to you?"

She silently groaned. "It's what's underneath that I have a problem with."

His eyes narrowed. "You don't know what's underneath. And don't go getting the idea you can find out."

His sarcasm put a snarl on Violet's face. "Just like I'd want to," she grumbled. "You must think I'm a complete idiot!"

"No. I think you're a liar."

Her face paled as fear lanced through her. Had he guessed, did he know she was hiding, running to escape?

"What have I lied about?" she whispered hoarsely.

His fingers curled around her chin, and his face dipped down to hers. "This," he murmured.

Confusion parted her lips, and Charlie was quick to take advantage. Like before, he hadn't planned to kiss her, but somehow he'd ended up doing it, anyway. But this time he realized he wasn't blinded by anger or caught off guard by something she'd said. This time he simply wanted her, and he needed to prove to her that she wanted him, too.

As Charlie's firm lips consumed Violet's she felt herself wilting like a sunflower in the broiling heat. Her head lolled back, and her shaky legs forced her to grab on to his shirt-front.

The thought of pulling out of his embrace never entered her mind. She was too caught up in the taste of him, the feel of his strong body crushed against hers. She'd never felt so lost, so wild, so totally female in her life. It was a heady, addictive feeling, and every inch of her sizzled with the need to be closer to him.

Long minutes passed before he finally ended the possession of her lips. By then Violet was too weak and breathless to even open her eyes.

"You know you'd like to get under my skin," he murmured against the smooth curve of her throat. "You'd like to know what makes me tick so you can push my buttons."

She didn't want to push his buttons, she thought wildly. She didn't want to be here in his house or his arms! But, oh, it was heaven to her starved heart.

"Is that what you're trying to do to me, push my buttons?" she asked breathlessly.

He nuzzled her nose and hair, then turned droopy eyes on her face. "No. I think Sam has become your whole life. I wanted to remind you that you're a woman."

"And I'm beginning to think you've been a Ranger so long you've forgotten how to be man!"

His nostrils flared and his hold on her chin tightened ever so slightly. "You like what I'm doing to you."

His lips hovered just above hers and his breath rippled like a warm, seductive breeze across her cheeks. Violet had to fight everything in her not to reach up, pull his head down and close the tiny gap between their lips.

"Maybe I do. But it takes more than that to be a real man."

She stayed in his arms long enough to see surprise flood his blue eyes, then she twisted out of his arms.

Stunned by her counterattack, Charlie could only stand there and watch her go out the screen door. Seconds later he could hear her in the backyard, talking to Sam. The air whooshed out of him like a deflated balloon.

What the hell did she know about men, he asked himself fiercely. What did she know about *him?* Nothing. And that was the way he was going to keep it. She might prick his ego, but that was a whole lot better than breaking his heart.

Chapter Six

Charlie never knew a child could talk so much in such a short span of time and ask questions for which he had no answers. He tried to tune him out and concentrate on the blooming sage, the grama grass, and the bright blossoms adorning the sticky choya. Late spring rains had blessed the high desert country of Lincoln county, and the evidence was all over the Pardee Ranch.

After he'd become a Ranger and started earning a living on his own, his father had allowed him to become a financial partner with him in the Pardee Ranch. It was a step Charlie was proud of, a decision he would never regret. Even though his life was in Texas serving as a Ranger, he could never forsake this land that had always been his home.

"Charlie, what is that? Is that a hawk?"

Sam's voice finally penetrated his thoughts, and he followed the line of the boy's finger, pointing through the windshield of the pickup. To the far right a bald, rocky mountain jutted into the clear New Mexico sky. Near the peak, a lone buzzard circled the barren formation, searching for even the smallest carcass.

"No," Charlie told him. "That's a buzzard. He's bigger than a hawk, and he eats rotten meat."

Violet shuddered. "Did you have to tell him that?"

He cast her a tired look. "Why not? It's something he'll learn in grade-school science."

"He's not yet in kindergarten, Charlie!"

Ignoring Violet's protest, Charlie glanced down at Sam's glowing face. "You'll just have a head start on all those other boys, won't you? You'll know all about nature before they ever learn to tie their shoes."

Sam giggled at the idea of being smarter than his classmates. "Tell me about the hawk, Charlie. What does he eat?"

"Well, that's the big difference between the hawk and the buzzard. The hawk catches his food live. Like mice or little rabbits or chipmunks, and then he eats it while it's still fresh. The buzzard is a lazy bird. He just flies around in circles, waiting for anything to die so he can eat it later."

Rapt with attention, Sam drank in every word, while next to the passenger window, Violet groaned and shook her head. Since her blow-up at Charlie yesterday, she'd been trying not to smother Sam and allow him to do more physical things outside. But she wasn't so sure he needed to learn science and geography and ranching. He was a baby. Her baby. This whole move from Amarillo had been to get him away from a possessive man. Now it looked as though Charlie was taking over.

"Could we ride Joe up there where that buzzard is now, Charlie?"

Charlie glanced once again at the sailing bird. "No. That's a little too rough up there. Joe would probably lose a shoe, and then his hoof would hurt and he'd limp."

"Why would it hurt?"

Charlie stifled a sigh. "Because it would get sore. Just like your feet would get sore if you tried to walk out there without your boots." He pointed to the rough range in front of them.

"But I wouldn't lose my boots, Charlie. I'd keep 'em on my feet."

"Be quiet, Sam. You're talking Charlie's ear off."

For the past fifteen minutes they had been traveling across an isolated part of the Pardee Ranch, and during the whole drive Charlie had wanted to tell the boy to hush. But now as he watched a dejected expression settle across his round cherub face, he berated himself for being selfish.

Sure, he'd come home to rest and get his mind off his work. But Sam was an innocent child. He couldn't help it because his mother's car had broken down or that he'd been forced to stay at Charlie's cabin.

Even if Sam's chatter got tiresome, Charlie found he couldn't be short or indifferent to the boy. It just wasn't in him. Roy hadn't raised him to be that sort of man. And hopefully the man Violet eventually married would treat Sam kindly. But would he love him? Would he love Violet?

Now where the hell had those questions come from? Charlie asked himself. It was enough that he was helping them get their car fixed and back on the road. He couldn't start wondering what would happen to them once they left here.

Annoyed with himself, he looked across to Violet's solemn face. She had avoided his questions last night about her home and acquaintances back in Amarillo. He was still wondering what her answers might have been if she hadn't bristled up. And he hadn't kissed her.

Kissed her! Damn it, he'd kissed Violet O'Dell more in the past forty-eight hours than he had any woman in the past twelve months. That's what he needed to be worried about. Not if the woman was going to be loved!

Five minutes later a group of buildings began to appear in the far distance. As they drew closer, Violet could see it was the Pardee Ranch. The house was a log structure similar to Charlie's cabin, except on a much larger scale.

Cottonwoods, poplars and piñon pine shaded the yard and grew along the banks of a shallow river flowing a few yards from the back of the house. To the north was an intricate maze of cattle pens and connecting barns.

Violet was both surprised and impressed by the size and condition of the ranch. She hadn't expected Charlie's parents to be so different. It made her wonder even more why Charlie chose to stay in Texas and be a Ranger rather than live here and help his father raise cattle.

Justine greeted them at the door, and once again the woman clutched Charlie to her.

"I'm glad you decided to come to supper," she said to them as they entered the house. "It gives me a reason to make a pig of myself. And Roy says I'm going to forget how to cook if I don't start doing more of it."

"Did Dad make it back from Las Cruces?" Charlie asked as they entered the house.

"No. He'll probably get back tomorrow evening."

She ushered them into the kitchen and insisted on Charlie and Violet having a glass of iced tea. For Sam, she poured a smaller glass of fruit punch.

While they all sipped their drinks, Justine caught Charlie up on the family news and some of the more difficult cases his father had been working on. Then, to Violet's surprise, she urged her son to take Sam down to the barn to see the horses while supper finished cooking.

"Trying to get rid of me?"

There was a faint teasing tone to Charlie's voice, but Violet got the impression he didn't want to go to the barn or take Sam with him. Most likely the latter, she figured.

Sam had already trailed after him for most of the day. She figured he was tired of the boy's company.

"At least until I get the chilies fried, or you'll be eating them before I can get them on the table."

From his perch on a barstool, Charlie glanced down at Sam, who was patting his knee like a bongo drum.

"I want to go see the horses, Charlie. Can we?"

As Charlie looked at the child's eager face, he wondered what his fellow rangers would think if they could see him now. Charlie Pardee playing stand-in daddy for a kid he hadn't even met until a few days ago. And Violet? What would the guys think about her? No doubt that she was beautiful and sexy. And that Charlie was smitten with her. But he wasn't. He damn well wasn't going to let himself be.

Everything about her said she was just like Angela. She didn't understand or even pretend to want to understand his being a lawman. He wasn't about to lay his heart open and have her laugh at him. That sort of humiliation a man could only take once in his life.

"I suppose we can. But don't start whining to ride," he warned Sam.

Justine frowned crossly at her son. "It wouldn't hurt if Sam wanted to ride Brown Sugar."

Charlie placed his empty tea glass on the bar and slid off the stool. "He's already been on Joe twice today," he pointed out to his mother.

Justine rolled her eyes, but Sam didn't seem a bit perturbed at Charlie. Grinning from ear to ear, the boy's little hand clamped around Charlie's forefinger and began to tug him toward the door.

"I remember a time when you were just a little older than Sam," Justine said to Charlie. "You rode all day long until your daddy would have to literally pull you out of the saddle."

In other words, Charlie needed to remember what it was to be Sam's age. Well, maybe he did need to remember. Maybe seeing all the guns and drugs and thieves and murderers and every crime committed against humanity had made him old and hard. But couldn't his mother understand he had to be that way?

Charlie had to be tough-hided as Violet had called him. He couldn't let the feel of Sam's soft little hand wrapped trustingly around his penetrate his armor. He didn't want the child's gamin grin and sparkling, innocent eyes to remind him how, if nothing in his life changed, he was going to miss having a son or daughter. He was going to live the rest of his life without a family of his own.

"When will supper be ready?" he asked impatiently.

"Whenever I yell off the back deck and let you know," his mother told him.

With a worried expression, Violet watched Charlie and Sam leave the kitchen through a back door that led onto a redwood deck.

"Charlie's going to think you really were trying to get rid of him," she said to Justine.

"I was."

Puzzled, she watched the woman tear Romaine lettuce into a big glass bowl. "But why? I thought you didn't get to see your son enough?"

Justine smiled at Violet. "I don't. But it will be good for him to spend time with Sam. He has no idea what being a father is like. Sometimes I don't think he ever wants to have children of his own."

"He told me as much," Violet admitted, then immediately felt like kicking herself. "I mean...well, he didn't exactly say he didn't want them. He just...intimated that he didn't believe he would ever have children."

Justine sighed wearily, but she didn't appear all that surprised or upset. "It's—frustrating seeing your child unhappy."

Violet left her seat at a small work table and joined Justine at the counter. "I know what you mean. All I want is for Sam to be happy."

She glanced reflectively at Violet. "Being a Texas Ranger is ruining my son. And I don't know what to do about it. I don't even know if there's anything I can do about it."

Violet was inwardly stunned by the woman's suggestions. True, Charlie Pardee didn't seem like the most joyous person in the world, but he had so much. Far more than Violet could ever dream of having. A big loving family. A respected job. What more did he want? Except a wife and children. And he'd already implied to Violet that he didn't want those.

"What do you mean?" Violet asked her. "You've been married to a sheriff for all these years. I figured you were proud that Charlie was a lawman, too."

For a moment Justine forgot the salad she was making. Her eyes lifted to the ceiling, then over to Violet. "Oh my dear, I am proud. Please don't get me wrong. Charlie worked hard to become a member of a group of lawmen that are loved and respected not only in Texas, but everywhere. His father and I are thrilled that he's accomplished that dream for himself. The trouble with Charlie is…he puts too much of himself into his job. He wants to make all things right, save and keep everyone from harm, solve every crime. Hasn't he talked about it to you?"

Violet's eyes widened. "Why no. He hasn't told me much of anything about his job. The first night after we met, I asked him if he liked being a Ranger, and he gave me some wishy-washy answer like 'being a lawman is just a way of life for me.'"

Justine sighed once more. "Well, he certainly spoke the

truth. Roy was a lawman even before Charlie was born. I guess he stamped it into his genes or something." She went back to ripping the lettuce leaves. "But Roy has the ability to stand back from his job and see it just for what it is…a job. For Charlie, being a lawman is his entire life."

Violet leaned her hip against the cabinets. She felt as if she ought to be helping Justine finish supper, but she got the idea the woman would rather have Violet as a listening post than a cooking partner.

"If Charlie's dream has always been to be a Ranger, he should be a contented man."

Justine nodded. "He should be. But he isn't. Surely you can see that."

Violet had seen a lot about Charlie in the past three days. At times he was curt and moody and downright arrogant. He thought he knew what she and Sam needed in their lives and he didn't take the subtle route of telling her. But oh, when he took her into his arms, he was the most perfect man she'd ever met.

"Well, since I only met your son a few days ago, I'm hardly one to say. I get the impression he isn't the let's-party-and-laugh sort."

Justine's head swung back and forth. "Charlie used to be a laid-back, happy-go-lucky guy. He was full of charm and humor. But little by little he's changed. First, I noticed his laughter was growing less and less frequent, then the smiles and teasing grins he always had for his family and friends began to vanish, too. Now he's as serious as a judge. And the only time he takes time off from his job is when his captain forces him to."

In spite of all the infuriating things Charlie had said to her, the man was doing her and Sam a great kindness by giving her a job and letting them stay in his cabin until her car was repaired. The idea that he might be a troubled man bothered Violet greatly. She knew what it was like to be full of pain and dejection.

"Maybe your son is just getting older and more settled."

"Charlie is nearly thirty. And he's always been a settled man. Even as a teenager he wasn't the sort to sow wild oats or flit from one job to the next. Far from it," she said, then laughed softly as though to tell herself she needed to lighten up. "Charlie always knew he wanted to be a Ranger."

As Violet watched the older woman dump a diced tomato into the salad bowl, she thought about all Justine had said.

"Does Charlie talk to you much about his job?"

Justine moved down the countertop to the gas range and stirred a pot of cheese sauce. "Some. He doesn't go into details. But Roy and I know something happened on a case a few months back that really affected him."

"He hasn't told you what it was?"

Justine shook her head. "Just that everything went wrong, and he felt as if it were all his fault."

Of all the things Justine had said about her son, this surprised Violet the most. Charlie seemed so self-assured, so confident. The last thing he appeared to be was a man possessed with guilt. She'd rather think a woman was his problem.

"Are you sure your son isn't troubled over a girlfriend? Or maybe he's gotten involved with a married woman and doesn't want you to know about it," Violet said.

Grimacing, Justine waved her hand through the air. "Oh well, Charlie's love life is a whole other story. The woman he wanted left him flat. Now he swears up and down..."

Suddenly her words trailed away and she looked at Violet as though something altogether different had struck her mind. Then with a shake of her head, she said, "I really shouldn't be telling you all this. Charlie wouldn't like it if he knew I was discussing him with you or anyone. Besides, you have enough problems of your own. And Charlie is going to have to figure his out on his own.''

She motioned for Violet to join her at the gas range. "Have you ever cooked *rellenos?*"

Violet was glad the woman was going to change the subject. She didn't want to hear about Charlie's troubles, or pain or sorrows. It was easier to let herself believe he was the tough, unshakable Ranger, who chased down the bad guys.

Shaking her head, Violet said, "No. My late husband didn't like Mexican food, so I never tried my hand at cooking it.''

Justine smiled broadly. "Well, I'm no chef. But I can show you a few things.''

A few minutes later the two of them were immersed in frying the long, breaded peppers when a light knock and a voice sounded behind them.

Violet turned to see a young woman about her own age walking into the kitchen carrying a covered plate. She was tall and slender, and her hair was a vibrant shade of red.

"Anna!" Justine exclaimed, then quickly went to her and kissed her cheek. "What are you doing here? I thought you'd already headed back to Santa Fe.''

Smiling, the young woman shook her head. "Not with out seeing Charlie first! I couldn't believe it when Mom told me he was home!" She handed Justine the covered plate. "Mom wanted you to have some of her carrot cake.''

"Chloe actually baked!" Justine exclaimed. "My sister never bakes.''

"I cajoled her into it," she said, then glanced to Violet who was still trying to tend to the frying peppers. "Hello," she said amiably. "Sorry for intruding. I'm Justine's niece.'' With a little laugh, she walked over to Violet. "Actually I'm her half sister, too. But legally I'm her niece.

She'll tell you the story sometime. Are you here with Charlie?''

This young woman was certainly forthright, but she was equally warm and friendly, and Violet liked her immediately.

"I guess you could say that."

"This is Violet, Anna. Isn't she beautiful?"

"Very!" She quickly snatched Violet up in an affectionate hug. "Oh, I'm so glad Charlie has finally found a woman. He's needed you for a long time!"

Violet's mouth fell open. "But I—"

"I know, don't tell me. He hasn't asked you to marry him or anything. But don't worry, he will. Charlie's never brought a woman home with him before. You *have* to be special!"

Violet turned her openmouthed stare on Justine. The older woman merely laughed.

"Forgive her. She's like my daughter, Caroline. A hopeless romantic."

Laughing, Anna kissed Justine's cheek again, then headed out the back door. "Sorry to dash in and out so quickly but I've got to be back in Santa Fe tonight."

"Charlie's down at the barn," Justine told her.

"That's where I'm headed. See ya!"

The kitchen seemed absurdly quiet after the door shut and the young woman was gone. Then suddenly Justine let out a little squeal and hurried to the deep-fry pot on the gas range.

"The peppers!"

"I've been watching them," Violet assured her. "I think they're okay."

With a pair of tongs Justine pulled up one of the peppers from the boiling oil. The breading was a beautiful golden brown. She looked at Violet and smiled. "They're perfect. I believe I've found a cooking partner."

* * *

Charlie was quiet at dinner, but Sam made up for it by reciting everything he'd seen and done down at the barn, including having Anna push him in the wheelbarrow and playing with three dogs.

Violet was immensely relieved to see her son enjoying himself, yet she was also worried. She had no idea what lay ahead of them once they left the Pardee Ranch. But wherever or whatever life they found, she knew it would surely be a letdown to Sam after all this.

After supper and the mess was cleared away, Charlie announced they had to be getting back to the cabin. As they prepared to leave, Justine gave Violet a ledger, a box of statements and receipts and a few simple instructions as to what she needed done.

"It won't be any problem at all," Violet assured the woman as they all walked outside to Charlie's pickup. "Thank you, Justine, for supper and the cooking lesson. And the job," she added, glancing down at the ledger and box she was carrying.

"You're more than welcome," she said, then looked over at her son, who was letting down the tailgate of the pickup. "I'm glad you came, too, Charlie."

"Thanks, Mom. Tell Dad I missed him," he said to his mother. "And that I'm taking Buster home with me for a few days. I need a watchdog around the place."

Charlie let out a low whistle. Three collie dogs suddenly appeared from the shadows and lined up at the back of the pickup.

"Maybe you should take Jane or Judy. The girls are much better watchdogs," Justine suggested.

Charlie shook his head and tried not to notice Sam was hugging the male dog's neck as if he were his greatest friend.

"No. The girls will go off hunting on their own. I'll take Buster. He minds better."

Laughing softly, Justine took hold of the collars on the other two dogs. "Obedience," she said to Violet. "You'll probably notice that's a necessary commodity to Charlie. He hasn't yet learned it doesn't work on women, though."

Charlie grunted at his mother's remark. "Maybe that's why me and women don't mix."

"I know," Justine replied fondly, but wearily. "You're the Lone Ranger."

Charlie kissed his mother's cheek. "He was a good guy, wasn't he?"

She smiled up at him and patted his arm. "Only the best. Like you."

Violet couldn't help but notice that he dismissed his mother's praise as though it bothered him or as if he felt as if he didn't deserve it.

"Load up, Buster," he said abruptly. "We've got to get home."

The dog instantly obeyed and jumped up into the pickup. Charlie fastened the tailgate back in place, and the dog's tail wagged wildly at being the chosen one.

"Buster goes for months without seeing you. But he never forgets you," Justine remarked as she watched the dog do his best to lick Charlie's hands.

Beside Violet, Sam began to jump up and down on the toes of his tennis shoes. "Charlie's taking Buster home with us! Buster is gonna go to our house, Mommy! Oh, boy!"

Home. Our house. Violet didn't know if Justine or Charlie noticed her son's choice of words, but she certainly did. And it made her more resolved than ever to leave as soon as she could. Sam had already had enough turmoil in his life without having to be uprooted once again.

Later that night after the three of them had made it back to the cabin and she'd helped Sam to bed, she found Charlie sitting in his regular spot on the front porch.

He glanced up with surprise when she offered him a cold glass of iced tea. "I didn't ask for this."

Did the man never have anyone simply offer him something without him asking for it first, she wondered. Did he never have a woman around to spoil him with little comforts?

"No," she agreed. "But it's still hot this evening. I thought you might enjoy it."

His eyes narrowed skeptically, and for a moment Violet felt like dumping the whole glass over his head.

"Don't worry," she drawled in a dry voice. "This isn't part of a seduction. It's not filled with some sort of aphrodisiac. It's simple tea, ice and sugar. I thought you especially needed the last ingredient."

"Are you this smart with all the men you're around?"

He plucked the glass of tea from the small tray, and Violet eased down into the chair next to him.

"I try not to be around men if at all possible."

He glanced at her to see if she was teasing. When he saw she wasn't, he said, "You're not a man hater."

If any woman had a right to hate men, it was Violet. But oddly enough she didn't hate them. She didn't even dislike them. She supposed there was still a part of her that hoped and yearned for a man to love her. Really love her with all his heart and soul. Not the halfhearted love Brent had given her.

She sighed. "No. I don't hate men. I guess I said what I did because…well, it's easier for me not to have to deal with them."

"Do you miss your husband?"

She couldn't believe he asked such personal things in such a blunt, forthright way. And once again she wondered if it was the Ranger in him or simply his no-nonsense personality that made him shoot questions at her.

"Sometimes. I miss Sam not having his father. And I

miss…'' Her words trailed wistfully away as her eyes
scanned the dark desert hills in front of them. "I miss the
way things used to be." She turned her gaze back on Charlie, and something in his face, some wounded, needy look
in his eyes drew her to him. And she realized she had to
share at least a part of herself with him. No matter what it
cost her in the end.

"Used to be?" he asked. "You mean before your husband was killed?"

She shook her head. "My…uh, my marriage was ending
when Brent was killed. A few weeks before his plane
crashed I'd gone to a lawyer and filed for divorce."

"I guess you'd think it impertinent if I asked why."

Violet stared into the glass of tea she was clutching with
both hands. Charlie would probably never see her the same
way again, but she couldn't stop her confession now.

"Brent had been having affairs. It was something that
started about the time Sam turned two. Of course, each time
I found out, he appeared to be remorseful about his behavior. He would always promise it would never happen again
and beg me to forgive him. But he…always seemed to find
another woman he couldn't resist."

Charlie didn't say anything for long moments. Violet
forced herself to swallow a mouthful of tea in hopes it
might ease the tightness in her throat.

"Why did you stay with him so long?" Charlie finally
asked.

One of Violet's slender shoulders lifted, then fell. "Because he was a very good father to Sam. And maybe—I
don't know—maybe a part of me kept hoping he really
would change."

"You say he was a good father, but what about being a
good husband to you?"

She turned a mocking look on him. "How could he be
a good husband when he was seeing other women? Or are

you one of those men who think it's okay and acceptable to keep a mistress on the side?''

"I think if a man is crazy enough to get married, he'd better make damn sure she's the only woman he'll ever want. In my opinion adulterers are lower than swine.''

She let out another long sigh. "Actually Brent was a good husband for the first few years we were married. But after Sam…I don't know what happened. I've asked myself, a thousand times over, what I did wrong, what I didn't have that made him seek out those other women. Over and over I blamed myself for not being woman enough to keep my husband home. I guess…I just wasn't capable of being a mother and a wife at the same time. But that's all over with now, and I guess I'll never know.''

Charlie watched as she took another long drink of tea, then place the glass on the floor beside her chair.

She believed the past was over and done with, but he could see it was still eating at her self-regard. What manner of man could have left this woman and turned to another, he wondered. What sort of bastard could have hurt her so deeply? And not just once but many times over?

"Have you ever thought that the trouble was with him? Not you?''

For as long as she could remember, the men in Violet's life had always blamed her for their weakness. To have Charlie, an unmoving mountain of a man, see and understand the other side of things was too much for Violet.

Her chin dropped against her chest as tears rolled down her cheeks.

"Violet? What's the matter?''

She couldn't speak. All she could manage to do was shake her head.

"Damn it, are you bawling?'' he asked gruffly.

She shook her head again and pressed her fingertips against her closed eyelids.

Charlie rose to his feet and stood in front of her chair. Violet's watery gaze fastened on the toes of his brown boots.

"No! I'm not bawling!" she muttered, but her voice was anything but normal.

Moments of awkward silence passed, and then she felt Charlie's big hand on the top of her head.

"You shouldn't be doing that, Violet."

His words and the awkward, yet tender stroke of his hand was too much for Violet. Jumping from her seat, she fell sobbing against his chest.

Stunned, he looked down at her small hands clutching the front of his shirt, her dark head buried against his chest. He'd never had any woman cling to him with such fierce need, and to have Violet turn to him, ask him for comfort, filled him with emotions he couldn't name or understand. He only knew he wanted her to stop crying, he wanted her to know that with him she would always be safe and protected. And loved.

His mind tried to block out the word even as his arms moved around her. No, he didn't love this woman, he assured himself. He simply wanted to ease her pain, to keep her safe, the way he should have kept Lupé Valdez safe.

"You shouldn't cry over him, Violet. He isn't worth it. Besides, he's gone. And you're very young. You'll find another man who'll be much better to you."

She lifted her face and looked up at him. "I don't want to find another man. After Brent, I don't think I could ever trust any man to be faithful to me."

And Charlie couldn't trust any woman to love him in spite of his job as a lawman. The thought twisted his lips to a wry line. "You don't want a man. And I don't want a woman. I've thought all along we were birds of the same feather."

Charlie believed she was like him? Sad and closed off and determined not to be loved? Surely she wasn't!

Wiping the last of her tears from her cheeks, she said, "I'm not like you, Charlie Pardee. You're a totally unhappy man."

"I'm not the one watering the porch floor with a flood of tears," he pointed out.

Violet realized it was time to let go of him, to back away and remember why she was here on this ranch and who he was. He wasn't a man who could help her. In the end he could only hurt her. Yet in spite of all that logic, she wasn't quite ready to end the sweet pleasure of having his body next to hers.

"No. You're too tough to cry," she said sadly, then tapped the tips of her fingers against the region of his heart. "But in here there's a bucket of tears."

His features grew stone smooth. "And I'm sure you think you're just the woman to dry them up?"

"I wouldn't be so vain to think any such thing. I just told you I couldn't keep Brent happy. I'd be crazy to think I could put a smile on your face. I wouldn't attempt to try."

He wanted to be relieved at her tough, indifferent remarks. But he wasn't. A part of him needed to believe she was standing here in his arms because she wanted him, because out of all the men in the world, he was the one who could ease her aching heart. It was damn crazy thinking on Charlie's part, but he couldn't seem to stop it.

Just as Violet was expecting some caustic remark from him, he shocked her by lifting her up and into the cradle of his arms.

Gasping, she flung her arm tightly around his neck. "Charlie! What are you doing?"

"I'm taking you to your bed. I think we've had enough conversation for tonight."

Chapter Seven

Sam was gone. The realization shocked the groggy cloud of sleep from Violet's head, and she bolted straight up in bed. It was well past sunup and the cabin was quiet. Was Charlie still in his bedroom asleep?

"Sam!"

Her call went unanswered and terror struck her heart. The last couple of days her son had grown comfortable with his temporary home in the desert. Had he gotten it in his head to wander off from the house to search for coyotes or some other such animal or bird Charlie had told him about?

Snatching up her cotton robe, she wrapped the thin material around her and raced through the house. Neither Charlie nor Sam were in the kitchen or any of the small connecting rooms.

Unmindful of her bare feet and flimsy covering, she hurried onto the front porch, then quickly stopped dead in her tracks. Sam and Charlie were out in the dusty yard tossing sticks for Buster to fetch.

The black-and-white Collie appeared to be grinning as

much as her son, and her heart wrung with bittersweet pain as she watched Sam hug the dog's neck. Charlie hadn't brought Buster over here to be a watchdog. He'd done it for Sam. Why? For her child? For her? Oh, dear God, she prayed, don't let me soften toward this hard lawman.

"Mommy!" Sam cried the moment he spotted Violet on the porch. "Come here and see how Buster can fetch! He's real smart. See?"

As Violet slowly moved down the steps, Sam reared back and threw the stick in his hand as far as he could. With a happy yelp, Buster immediately raced after it.

By the time Violet had reached the two of them, the dog had returned. Sam took the stick from the dog's grinning mouth and gave the animal another loving squeeze.

"Isn't he beautiful, Mommy? See how much he likes me? Charlie says you can tell when a dog likes you if he licks you and wags his tail."

Buster's tongue was lapping at Sam's round little cheeks, and Violet couldn't help but smile at the picture the two of them made. "If that's the case, then I think Buster likes you a lot."

The dog began to bark and taunt Sam to throw the stick again. As the child and animal played the game once more, Violet turned to Charlie.

"I woke up and found Sam gone from the bed. I was frightened he'd wandered off in the hills."

His blue gaze drifted languidly up and down the length of her, and Violet couldn't help but wrap the thin robe more tightly around her body.

"You don't have much trust in your son, do you?"

She tried not to bristle at his question. "Normally, I do. But he's a child. The desert might lure him to leave the safety of the yard and go exploring."

"I've explained the dangers to him. He knows not to go off unless I'm with him."

Her mouth fell open, and his eyes settled on her parted lips.

"And you think simply telling him that is enough?" She snorted as she tossed back her tangled hair. "You don't know anything about children. Their minds can change in an instant."

Charlie wished his mind could change that quickly. The sight of her naked face and the fact that she was wearing next to nothing under her robe made him want to take up right where he'd been last night on the porch. With her in his arms.

"You're right. I don't know much about kids," he conceded. "But you should give Sam more credit. He's a smart boy."

He was a smart child, Violet had to agree, and she was only being testy with Charlie because she'd woken to such a fright. Sighing, she passed a hand over her face. "I know. And I'm trying not to…hang on so tightly. But when I woke up and saw him gone I…well, I was scared."

A few steps away Sam and Buster were playing tag, and it was easy to see the dog was loving the game as much as her son.

"Charlie, can I race Buster to the barn and back?" Sam asked.

Charlie glanced at Violet, then looked down at the boy, who'd trotted over to his side.

"Your mother is here now, you should ask her permission."

Sam instantly latched on to Violet's hand and tugged eagerly. "Can I, Mommy?" His finger pointed toward the barn which was less than a hundred feet away. "Just to the fence and back?"

Violet nodded, and boy and dog took off at a run, across the barren yard. She watched the two of them for a moment, then glanced knowingly at Charlie. "You brought Buster over here for Sam. Not for a watchdog."

His face stoic, he slowly folded his arms across his chest. "Now why should my motives be entering your mind? It doesn't matter why I brought Buster home with me. Or you and Sam. You're here. For a little while."

For a little while. Like a slap, his words shocked her back to reality, and it dawned on her how right he really was. It didn't matter why he was being kind enough to house and feed her and her child. He wasn't planning anything long-term. And neither was she. But deep inside her she knew saying goodbye to Charlie Pardee wasn't going to be an easy thing to do.

The wind blew her dark, tumbled hair across her face, and she was suddenly reminded that she'd only climbed out of bed a few minutes ago, the same bed that Charlie had carried her to last night, then whispered good-night.

Looking at him now, it was hard to believe he'd held her, comforted in a way no man ever had. From the closed expression on his face, Violet got the impression he regretted those few moments. Or at least he never wanted to repeat them again. The idea saddened her. But she squared her shoulders and hoped none of what she was feeling showed on her face.

"Have you had breakfast?"

"I gave Sam some juice and I had coffee."

"I'll go make us something," she said, then walked slowly back to the house.

Violet was on her way to the bedroom to change her clothes when the sound of a vehicle caught her attention. Curious, she walked to the living room and looked out the screen door.

Charlie's mother was pulling up in the same pickup she'd arrived in the other morning. Violet's first inclination was to hurry to the bedroom and dress so Justine wouldn't find her wearing only a thin bathrobe. But after a second glance it became clear the older woman had no intentions of coming in and staying for a visit.

The older woman handed Charlie a small square of paper, spoke briefly to him, then said a few words to Sam and climbed back into her pickup.

After she'd started the engine, Charlie leaned his head inside the open window and said something to his mother that caused the woman to shake her head, then he stepped back and lifted his hand in farewell.

Justine's truck was already headed back down the road when Charlie started to the house. Violet didn't bother to move. She expected he'd already seen her standing there. It would look ridiculous to try and hide her curiosity now.

"Is something wrong?" she asked Charlie as he stepped into the house.

He looked at her oddly. "No. Why would you think something was wrong?"

Because things had been wrong in Violet's life for so long now she could hardly think anything else.

She shrugged, hoping Charlie wouldn't pick up on her uneasiness. "I was...just surprised your mother didn't stay for a while."

He unfolded the square of paper his mother had given him, glanced at it, then stuffed the note into the pocket of his red T-shirt. Violet wondered what kind of message he could have gotten that his mother couldn't give him verbally.

"She had things to do. She's expecting Dad home this afternoon. Even after all these years a night apart is torture for them."

A night apart from Brent had been torture for Violet, too. But for totally different reasons. Once she'd learned he'd been unfaithful, she knew his nights away meant he was spending time with another woman.

"I think that's wonderful," she murmured.

Charlie's gaze slid from her face, down the creamy line of her neck to where her robe made a vee between her breasts. The hint of soft cleavage stirred unbidden visions in his head and he could only imagine what it would be like to come home from a stakeout and find her in his bed.

Violet's green eyes scanned his face. "You say that like...you're almost jealous."

Shrugging, he turned away from her. "I guess I am. A little."

"But they're your parents! You should be thrilled they're so in love."

He turned around to face her, and Violet was struck by the emptiness on his face. "I didn't say I was jealous of them. I'm jealous of what they have," he said, then let out a bitter snort. "Damn stupid of me, isn't it?"

It wasn't stupid. It was sad and human and something she wasn't expecting from Charlie. "Why is it stupid? I think everyone wants to be loved and wanted and needed."

He turned his back to her, and Violet watched his shoulders lift and fall as though he were heaving out a deep breath. And at that moment she knew she'd been right last night when she'd told Charlie his heart was full of tears.

The unexpected need to comfort him was stronger than the inner warning to keep her distance from the man. She moved over to him and placed her palm against his back. The contact caused his head to twist around in surprise and his blue eyes caught her gaze.

"What are you doing?"

The blunt question should have put her off, but she kept her hand against the hard warmth of him, anyway. "Trying to tell you that you're not alone."

He made another mocking sound in his throat. "Hell, I've got a family as huge as Texas. I'm not alone. And even if I was, it wouldn't make me unhappy. I like my own company.''

''If that's the case, then you shouldn't be jealous of the closeness your parents share.''

''I'm not. Really. I don't even know why I said that. And I sure as hell don't know why you're continuing to harp on it!'' he said sharply.

Violet didn't know what was wrong with her or what it was inside her that made her want to push him, goad him to open up to her. She didn't need to know what was underneath this man's tough hide. If she really knew she might just begin to care. And that would be a disastrous mistake.

''Are Texas Rangers permitted to lie?''

His face like dark slate, Charlie whirled around and grabbed her by the shoulders. ''You don't know anything about me or the way I have to live! If you did you would see that I'll never have the chance to be like my father. To have a woman who understands and supports his need to be a lawman.''

''There are thousands of women who have lawmen for husbands. If you're using your job as an excuse for not being able to hold on to a woman, then you're lying to yourself.''

A snarl exposed his white teeth. ''Oh, yeah. I'm sure you'd be more than ready to hitch yourself to another man who was gone three-fourths of the time. I'm sure you'd feel real secure with a relationship like that.''

The awful sarcasm in his voice was enough to make her want to slap him. Yet she didn't. She couldn't even bring herself to be angry with him. Because there was a scary truth to his words. And they both knew it.

Unable to pull her gaze from the grip of his, she stared at him, and her voice quavered with emotion when she spoke. "Maybe *I* couldn't. But there's a woman out there who could."

The mockery on his face deepened. "Sure. And what kind of woman would she be, Violet? Is she beautiful and vibrant and sexy and smart? Is she someone I'll want to spend the rest of my life with?"

For some odd reason Violet didn't want to think of him spending his life with any woman. She didn't want to imagine some other woman in his arms, smiling up at him, kissing his lips and making love to him. The proprietary feeling was like a lance of fear driving right through her. She wasn't the woman he was needing. She couldn't let herself be. If he knew of the horrible things she'd run from, he wouldn't simply frown upon her, he'd probably want to arrest her!

"I have no idea what kind of woman turns you on. Besides, you've already told me several times you're not looking for one."

A sudden light gleamed in his eyes, and Violet's heart shoved itself into overdrive as he moved closer. "What if I said you turned me on?" he asked, his voice low and gruff.

"I'd say you were a man who was either bored or didn't know what he wanted."

To her amazement he chuckled low in his throat. "Right at this moment I know exactly what I want. It's the afterward that has me all tangled up."

Before she could digest the meaning behind his words, Charlie's fingers slid to where the edge of her robe met the skin of her collarbone. The intimate contact caused Violet to draw in a sharp breath.

"You don't know...what you're saying or doing," she murmured in protest.

A mocking grin curved his lips. "Oh, I know, and I also

realize I'm damn crazy. But that doesn't stop what I'm feeling."

Violet couldn't block the next question from passing her lips. "What are you feeling?"

From the corner of her eye she could spot Sam out the living room window. Thank goodness he was still safely playing with Buster and totally oblivious of the two adults inside the house.

Charlie's eyes roamed her face as his fingers slipped lower. "It should be obvious to you. I'd like to make love to you. For a long, long time."

Heat suffused her body and turned her face a warm pink. "What's stopping you?" she asked boldly.

His blue eyes widened just a fraction, and then his hand was suddenly on her breast, circling its roundness, then cupping it in his palm.

"I thought you would," he said. Then, before she could respond, his head dipped and he was gently biting her nipple through the thin fabric of her robe.

Stunned motionless, Violet couldn't move away. And then she didn't want to, as a hot flood of need filled her up and left every muscle in her body lax and helpless to his touch.

His mouth eventually deserted her breast, and she could feel his warm rapid breaths against her as his lips skimmed a trail over the bare skin exposed by her gaping robe. "You would stop me, wouldn't you? If I lifted you in my arms and carried you to my bed?"

Would she? The way Violet felt at this moment she wasn't sure she could deny him anything. No man had ever made her feel so heady and reckless, so much a woman. It was a powerful feeling that urged her to forget the logic in her head and lose herself in the magic of his touch. But a part of her knew making love to Charlie was akin to an alcoholic reaching for a bottle. The first drink would never be enough.

"Sam is just outside. He could come in any minute."

His lips moved across her cheek and hovered over hers. "Is that the only thing stopping you?"

Her knees began to quiver, and she realized her hands were gripping his forearms. "No. I..."

He didn't let her finish. Suddenly she was crushed against his chest, and his lips were consuming hers. Not with anger, but with white-hot desire.

She was clinging weakly to him by the time he let her breathe again. The first thing she saw when her eyelids fluttered open was the glitter of his mocking smile.

"Now who's lying?" he asked.

She shoved against his chest. It was like pushing against a six-foot boulder. "Let me go! You don't want me. *Any* woman would satisfy you. Just so long as you could keep her under your thumb and know she'd stay safely at home while you were out playing with your six-shooter."

In the short time she'd known him, Violet had never seen his face go so hard and threatening. "What would you know about it?"

The cool softness of his voice left her insides shivering. "Justine said your woman left you. And from all you've just told me, I can make my own deductions. Your job comes first, and anything else is just an afterthought."

"Angela was never *my* woman. And what could you know about my job?"

Her chin lifted a fraction. "Not much. Why don't you tell me?"

He studied her with icy calmness. "Because I don't want to," he said, then turned his back to her and headed out of the room. "Go make breakfast. I've got a phone call to make."

Violet stared after his retreating back as the weight of

rejection enveloped her like a heavy, black cloud. The only thing Charlie wanted from her was a plain ole romp in the hay. Nothing more. In his own way he was just as selfish as her father had been, as Brent had been and then, later, Rex. Now Charlie. Was it her lot in life to be used by men?

Doing her best to swallow away the raw tears in her throat, Violet headed to the kitchen to make breakfast.

Violet lifted her head and flexed her aching shoulders. She'd been sitting at the kitchen table for nearly two hours, pouring over the ledger and the checks and receipts Justine had given her nearly two weeks ago.

She liked keeping books for Charlie's mother. The older woman was so laid-back and undemanding that Violet had to remind herself she was actually working for her. But each night after Sam went to bed and Violet pulled out the ledger, she was haunted by all she'd left behind in Amarillo.

By now Rex had to be enraged over her leaving and taking his grandson with her. He'd probably already sent some of his hired thugs out to search for her. Thank God they hadn't caught up to her yet.

With a weary sigh, she rubbed her eyes and glanced down at the open pages of debits and credits. Justine's was a simple bookkeeping system, one that a high school student could easily understand. Rex's books at the O'Dell Packing Company had been a different story. Everything was on computer file, where hundreds of entries were made during a work week.

There were times Violet wished she wasn't so good with numbers. Otherwise she might never have picked up on the fact that Rex and his friends had been running stolen cattle through the slaughterhouse.

She pinched the bridge of her nose and closed her eyes as she recalled the moment she'd confronted her father-in-law about her discovery. At first he'd laughed at her accusations. But the moment she'd informed him she was going to contact the law, he'd turned dangerous and threatening.

Furiously, he'd told Violet he wasn't about to let her take him down over a few measly head of cattle. And he had no intentions of allowing her to leave with Sam. He wanted his grandchild near him and he'd go to any means to see that he kept him. Even blackmail.

The agonizing thought propelled Violet out of her chair, and she walked barefoot over to the screen door leading out to the backyard.

She didn't know how Rex had found out about her brush with the law back in Georgia, but he had and he wouldn't hesitate to use it in a custody battle over Sam. True he might not win. But a judge would hardly look at a mother favorably when she'd been caught attempting to hawk stolen goods. Of course she hadn't known anything her father had given her to take to the pawn shop had been stolen. She'd done it to please him, to help him because he was broke and hungry. Violet's mistake had been in thinking her father had been hungry for food rather than liquor.

Forcing the humiliating scrape to the back of her mind, she pressed her nose against the screen and gazed out at the summer night. The sun had fallen behind the mountains more than two hours ago, but Charlie still wasn't home. Since the morning his mother had brought him a message, he'd gradually been away from the cabin more and more every day. She didn't know what he was doing. And she hadn't asked. But she wondered. And she missed him. Terribly.

The sound of a truck became a steady hum in the distance, and then she heard it pull to a stop in front of the house. She told herself to stay put. If it was Charlie, she didn't want to rush to the door and give him the idea she was eager to see him. Since he'd taunted her about making love with him, she'd purposely stayed a safe distance from him and kept her thoughts to herself.

"What are you doing still up?"

She turned around to see him standing in the doorway leading into the kitchen. His jeans and blue chambray shirt were covered with dust, and beneath the brim of his straw hat, she could see lines of exhaustion on his face.

Telling herself he would resent any sort of comfort she might offer him, she jammed her hands down in the pockets on her shorts and moved back to the table where she'd left her bookwork.

"Working on your mother's ledger."

He frowned. "She doesn't expect you to do all that in a few short days. Besides, it's only for tax purposes. She won't need it until the middle of August."

Violet began to gather the papers together and stuff them back into a box. Behind her, Charlie went to the refrigerator and pulled out a soft drink.

"That's more than six weeks away. I won't be here the middle of August. And, anyway, I don't like to leave work undone." She carried the box and the ledger over to a cabinet and safely stored them away. When she turned back, Charlie had taken a seat at the table. She didn't know why it felt so good to look at him or why it was unbearable to think of the time she would eventually leave here.

"Speaking of work," she told him, "this afternoon I finished hanging the last bit of wallpaper in the bathroom."

With a tired groan, he propped his dusty boots out in front of him. "You should have waited until I could help you. I don't expect you to do things like that on your own."

"If I waited on you, things would never get done."

"Getting in a hurry to leave?"

With each day that passed, leaving was becoming more and more on Violet's mind. Her car was being repaired, and though she hadn't done enough work to warrant the cost of repairing her engine, she was considering giving the mechanic a check on her bank account back in Amarillo.

Rex would eventually receive her bank statement in the mail and the canceled check would be a giveaway as to where she'd been staying. But by then she could be long gone. Maybe even all the way to northern California. It might be worth the chance if it would get her and Sam out of this house sooner. Because each day, each hour, that passed told her she and her son were becoming far too entrenched in this Texas Ranger's life.

"Maybe," she said quietly.

He studied the bottle of cola in his hand. "What's the matter? You don't like the jobs I've been giving you?"

She turned her back to him and picked up a cracker from a basket on the counter. The little paint and papering jobs he'd given her to do so far had been next to nothing. It was him and her growing feelings for him that she didn't like.

"I don't mind work. I just...feel the need to get back on the road. We need to find a place soon. I want Sam to be settled into a home and neighborhood before he enrolls in kindergarten. Starting school is an important time for a child, I want him to be happy and secure."

"If you're so concerned about Sam's security, why the hell did you run off from Amarillo in the first place?" he growled at her.

His unexpected question shocked Violet and she whirled around to face him.

"Because I..." Her mouth opened, but the words jammed in her throat. She couldn't tell this man anything! If she told him she'd discovered her father-in-law was a thief and had done nothing to stop it, he would consider her just as guilty as Rex! He'd certainly want to know why she hadn't gone to the law before now. But she couldn't tell him. The whole thing was too humiliating, and she doubted he would believe her innocence, anyway.

She swallowed and glanced away from him. "I didn't like living with my father-in-law," she said bluntly.

Charlie didn't say anything as he studied her for long moments. "Did you always live with him or has it been just since your husband died?"

She let out a small sigh. "Brent and I always lived with his father. He had a huge house, and his wife had died years before. When we first married it seemed the sensible thing to do. The house was nice, and Sam had plenty of space to play. Rex didn't really stick his nose into our business. But things changed after Brent died." Frowning, she shook her head. "I don't know why I'm telling you all this. It's not important."

"It was important enough to make you run."

Run. Funny that he should use that particular word, because that's exactly what she'd done. Run as hard and fast as she could.

She didn't make any sort of reply. She was afraid to. Something about Charlie brought everything to the surface in Violet, and she knew it wouldn't take much for her to break down and tell him the whole nasty lot of her past life.

"Did your father-in-law make sexual advances toward you? Is that the part you're not telling me?" Charlie moved closer.

Her heart cringed. She wanted to believe Charlie was asking because he actually cared, but common sense told her he simply saw her as his job. "What makes you think there's a part I'm not telling you?"

He snorted. "I've known there was another part of you since the first day I met you."

The certainty in his voice both irked and frightened Violet. Why did the man have to be so intuitive? But moreover, why had he ever brought her home with him in the first place?

She twisted around to find him only inches away. Her heart nearly stopped as she looked into his blue eyes, the male scent of him enveloping her.

"If you thought I was lying to you, why did you ever offer to help me?"

He inched closer until his thighs were very nearly brushing against hers. "I didn't say you were lying. You're just holding something back."

He was too close for comfort in more ways than one. But like always when he was near, she couldn't seem to tear herself away from him. Physically or mentally.

She drew in a deep breath in hopes it would calm her racing heart. "I told you I didn't want to live with my father-in-law anymore. He...wasn't coming on to me or anything like that. It was Sam that I was worried about. Rex wanted to take complete control of him. He wanted him to be his son instead of mine."

Charlie's calculating gaze roamed her face. "The man just lost his son. I can see how he'd want to use Sam to replace him."

Relieved, she nodded. "That's exactly what was happening."

"I suppose you told him all this?"

She nodded once again. "It didn't do any good. Rex is...a bully of a man. He gets what he wants no matter who he has to run over in the process."

"Sounds like you don't like him."

She groaned. "Like him? I loathe him. I hope I never have to lay eyes on him again."

"Did you rely on him for money?"

Suddenly his nearness was bothering Violet far more than his questions. Even though he wasn't exactly touching her, she could feel the heat and the hardness of his body, and everything inside her wanted him with a vengeance.

"No. I have money of my own."

This caused his brows to lift, and she knew she'd said too much.

"I mean, Brent's insurance left me secure."

His fingers reached out and stroked her bare upper arm. "Then why the need for a job to get your car going? You told me you didn't have enough money."

Her green eyes darkened with apprehension, and she nervously licked her lips. "I don't. Not...with me. It's...in a bank in Amarillo."

His fingertips stilled against her skin. "If you were a suspect, I'd have to say you're not sounding too convincing."

That's exactly what the sheriff back in Georgia had said when she'd tried to explain that the items she'd taken to the pawn shop had belonged to her drunken father and not her.

Groaning, her eyes dropped to the middle of his chest. "I know I sound crazy. But...I don't want to write any checks until I'm forced to. Rex will get my bank statement in the mail and then...well, he'll know where I am."

"Hellfire, Violet, you make the man sound like he's a demon who's out to kill you."

Rex would never harm her physically. He wasn't the sort. As far as Violet was concerned, the pain he could inflict on her would be far worse than death. Without Sam she wouldn't have anything to live for.

She tried to laugh and lighten the moment. "If I sound that way it's because I left angry. Rex would never do anything so violent."

As Charlie touched her warm skin and watched an array of lights and shadows play in her eyes, he couldn't help thinking how Lupé Valdez had once been as certain about her relative as Violet was now.

Charlie had only known Lupé briefly. He hadn't been attracted to her in a man-to-woman way. Yet he had admired her courage and her desire to see her drug-running uncle put behind bars. As the Texas Rangers and other law enforcers drew closer to an arrest, Charlie had talked her into going to Fort Worth to give a deposition, and he'd promised she would be under constant surveillance and no harm would come to her. He'd left her in a motel, safely guarded by two local policemen. But she'd never seen the sun come up the following morning. Lupé had been killed, and Charlie had taken full blame.

"Charlie? What's the matter? Are you—"

Violet's voice finally penetrated his tormented thoughts, and he stared at her blankly. "What did you say?"

Puzzled and wary, she repeated, "I was asking you if something was wrong. Are you feeling okay? You look like you've just seen the gates of hell."

He had. He'd seen Lupé's lifeless body, but the face had changed to Violet's pale, beautiful features. Rocked by the image, he grabbed her by the shoulders and shook her until her dark hair fell wildly over her face.

"Violet, you'd better not be lying to me. If this codger is dangerous I want to know it, and I want to know it right this instant!"

The growl of his voice filled the little kitchen, and she was glad Sam was asleep. Charlie's behavior would probably frighten him.

"I just told you!" she flung at him. She placed her hands against his chest and tried to lever a few inches between them. But her efforts were futile. If anything he was closer, his chest and hips pressing her back against the cabinets.

"You haven't told me everything," he countered. "You're scared of this man. I can see it on your face."

Yes, she was scared, but not for the reason Charlie was thinking.

"I'm not," she denied. "I just want to...avoid him."

His hands left her shoulders and stabbed into her hair. With his fingers pressed against her scalp, he held her face up to his. "You're lying. You want to do more than avoid the man! You're planning to put several states between you!" His grip against her scalp suddenly eased, and so did his expression. "Violet," he softly coaxed, "if you're frightened he's going to hurt you, tell me. I'm in a position to help you. And I will."

"Why?"

He looked taken aback. "Why? Because you need help. Because it's my job."

"Oh."

The one word came out like a defeated sigh, and he studied her with new eyes. "You didn't think it was for personal reasons, did you?"

"Maybe. I don't expect you to go around getting this close to all the women you find in peril."

His brows lifted and Violet watched his lips move as he spoke. "I've come in contact with a lot of people since I've become a Ranger. Many of them were women. But none of them have made me feel as foolish as you do."

Somehow her thudding heart kicked into an even faster rhythm. "Foolish?"

His hands slid down to cup her face, and Violet felt everything inside her wilt as his tough palms pressed against her skin.

"I can't be in the same room without touching you," he said huskily. "Right now I want to toss you onto the kitchen table and make love to you."

The image his words created caused heat to flare deep inside Violet. "Maybe it's not Rex I should be worried about,'' she said shakily. ''Maybe you're the one who's liable to wind up hurting me.''

''How could you think I would ever hurt you?'' he murmured. ''I'd kill any man who tried to.''

She began to tremble, and her fingers clutched the folds of his dusty cotton shirt. ''Why? Because it's your job?''

No, he silently answered. It wasn't his job that was making him so fiercely protective and possessive of her. It was his heart. He loved Violet O'Dell. He didn't want to acknowledge it, but the revelation shot through him like a flaming arrow. He couldn't ignore the thrill rushing through him. Nor the awful sense of foreboding quickly following it. Violet wasn't going to return his love. She'd be leaving soon. And even if she wasn't, she'd already been soured by a cheating man.

''Has my mother been…telling you things?''

His question caught Violet off guard, and her eyes widened with surprise. ''Why, no. What sort of things? About you?''

Everything inside Charlie wanted to forget caution and simply crush her to him, kiss her lips and whisper how much he adored her. His heart was sure it was the right thing to do. But the logic in his brain screamed he should keep his feelings to himself. He'd already been hurt and humiliated by one woman. Why give Violet the chance to do it again? Especially when he knew his job and her mistrust in men would never work. Each time he walked out of the house, she'd be thinking he was with another woman.

''About me and my job.''

Violet's eyes fell guiltily from his. ''Only that it was making you unhappy. She thinks you devote too much time to it. She believes you're so busy trying to keep everyone else safe and protected you're neglecting your personal life.''

A month ago. Even a week ago, Charlie would have been

infuriated hearing his mother say such things, especially to Violet. But now he could only wonder how she'd seen so much about him that he hadn't seen until a few moments ago.

"Charlie? Are you angry? Your mother was only talking out of concern. Because she wants you to be happy."

Realizing he'd been staring off in space, he glanced down to see Violet looking up at him. Her pretty features were marred with a worried frown.

"I'm not angry. I'm just amazed."

She shook her head in confusion. She'd never seen him look as he did at this moment. As if he'd been gazing at the horizon and finally figured out what was there. "Amazed? I...what do you mean?"

Frustrated by the barrage of emotions sweeping over him, he groaned and turned away from her. "She's been telling me the very same thing for more than a year now, and I always angrily cut her off. I thought my captain didn't understand me, either. But all this time it was me who couldn't see."

She could hear self-recrimination in his low voice. The sound urged her to step forward and place her hand against his back. "What couldn't you see? That you don't like being a Ranger?"

His shoulders lifted and fell as he breathed deeply, and then he whirled around with a suddenness that startled Violet. He grabbed the sides of her waist and stared at her with such intensity she grew dizzy.

"No, thank God. I was beginning to wonder if maybe I'd wasted eight years of my life. But now I realize—"

The abrupt halt of his words left her uneasy and almost afraid to prompt him to go on. But she had to. She had to know what had caused the dawning light in his eyes.

"What?"

He shook his head, and his mouth went dry with fear. "Nothing."

She frowned. "Charlie, you're not making any sense at all. You're acting strange. What have you been doing today?"

An endearing little grin cocked one corner of his mouth. "Falling in love with you, Violet."

Chapter Eight

"Love isn't something you joke about, Charlie!"

The engaging grin instantly disappeared and his expression turned gravely serious.

"I'm not joking, Violet."

Violet didn't know how stark fear and ecstatic joy could rush through her at the same time, but they did. For the next few moments all she could manage to do was stare at him in stunned fascination.

"You must be. You have to be," she whispered, then, as the full meaning of what he was saying hit her, she struggled out of his arms and hurried across the room.

Charlie went after her. Once he'd reached her, he took her by the upper arm. "Look, Violet, I wasn't planning on blurting this out to you. I...hell, I didn't know until just a minute ago what my feelings for you were turning into. But I do now."

Her eyes were full of skepticism as they lifted to his. "Do you know how crazy that sounds, Charlie? One minute you don't even know what you feel for me and then the next you say you love me. I thought only oversexed high school boys spouted things like that.''

Her doubt angered him, and his hold on her arm tightened. ''Damn it, Violet, I wasn't asking for this. And I sure as hell wasn't looking for it.''

Her nostrils flared as she jerked her arm from his grip. ''You sure sound like a man who's deliriously in love,'' she said cuttingly.

''I didn't say I was happy about it,'' he snapped.

Maybe it was his anger or the shocked look on his face that made Violet realize he really had been telling her the truth, and the whole idea left her trembling and wondering where to turn next.

''Then why did you tell me? To get me in your bed?''

He mouthed a curse word. ''I've had two weeks to get you in my bed. And I didn't need to tell you I love you to do it. All I had to do was throw away my morals.''

She knew he was right. If he'd really pressed her, she doubted very much that she could have resisted him. She'd never felt such a strong physical attraction for any man. But it was Charlie and his honorable beliefs—Charlie, the Durango Kid—who'd decided not to take advantage of her.

Suddenly swamped with emotion, she covered her face with her hands and turned away from him. ''I don't know what you want me to do. Or say,'' she mumbled.

Both his hands dropped to her shoulders, and his fingers kneaded her soft skin. ''I guess…I need to know if my feelings mean anything to you.''

Instantly Violet twisted around to face him. ''Yes! Of course they do! But—'' She broke off with an anguished groan. ''I can't…let anything grow between us.''

''Why? Because I'm a Texas Ranger?''

Yes! But not in the sense he was thinking. Oh, Lord, she prayed, how could she explain without hurting him or herself. She couldn't let him find out about Rex! Or the trouble she'd been in back in Georgia. She'd rather die first.

"Charlie, if you're thinking I'm like that other woman, I'm not. At least, I understand that your job is important to you and that any woman you choose would have to share you with it. But I...right now my life is...crazy. It has been for a long time. That's why you found me on the highway like you did. I've got to make a place for myself and my son before I can ever think about letting a man into my life."

"I could help you find that place, Violet. For you and Sam."

She began to tremble. Every fiber of her heart wanted to believe and imagine she could have a life with Charlie. She didn't know when the idea had taken root or why she was just now admitting it to herself. The only thing she did know was that she could never let it happen. Not even for a short while. Charlie was an honest, dedicated lawman. To hook up with her would only bring him embarrassment and possibly even trouble. She couldn't do such a thing to him.

With a tormented groan she stepped around him and hurried through the screen door. The night had finally cooled, and a silver half-moon lit the wide sky above her. She stared up at it as she breathed deeply and tried to calm her raging senses.

The sound of the door softly banging behind her announced that Charlie had followed her. Somehow she'd known he would. She hadn't come out here expecting to escape, just to find enough space to breathe and back away from him. If she could.

"Do you always run from everything?"

She glanced over her shoulder at him and a pain of regret stabbed her right in the middle of the chest. Why couldn't she have met him years ago? she wondered. Long before Brent had ever taught her about betrayal and broken hearts.

"I'm not running. I'm thinking."

He stepped closer. "About what?"

"You. I thought you never wanted to marry or have children," she said pointedly. "You said your job was your life."

"I know I said all of that. But it isn't the way I feel now."

She argued, "Those sorts of ideas can't change overnight, Charlie."

He took her hand and led her down the steps. Beneath the cottonwood was an old wooden bench worn smooth from years of use. He nudged Violet onto the seat, then sat down close beside her.

The night breeze was blowing, and just above her head the leaves rustled softly. It was a soothing sound, and this place was a peaceful spot in the desert mountains. But now she had to leave it and Charlie for good. She couldn't continue to stay. It wouldn't be fair to either of them.

After a moment he took her hand and she looked at him with tortured eyes. "Violet," he said gently, "for the past year I've been...well, I haven't exactly been myself. My job has consumed me. But I've let it. I wouldn't take time off even when it was offered to me. I wouldn't even come home to see my family. I was afraid that if I did something bad would happen."

"Bad would happen," she repeated with a puzzled shake of her head. "You mean something to your fellow Rangers?"

With a shrug he glanced away from her. "Partly. Or some victim we'd been working with. Or maybe a witness or anyone who'd ever met me on the job and needed me."

"That's quite a big area for one man to cover."

He let out a heavy breath. "I know. Now."

Violet didn't urge him to say more. She sat quietly beside

him, waiting, wondering what was going on in his head, what had been going on for all these months.

He reached for her other hand, and when she allowed him to take it, he looked at her. "For a long time I've been feeling pretty guilty."

The desolate expression on his face tore at her, and she desperately wanted to make it vanish, to see him smile and hear him laugh. "'Guilty,'" she echoed softly. "I can't imagine you being guilty of anything. Except maybe a little arrogance," she tried to tease.

He didn't smile. Rather he closed his eyes and tightened his hold on her hand. "I caused a young woman to die, Violet. A young woman like you. With her whole life ahead of her."

Violet gasped. "Oh Charlie, no! I don't believe that."

His eyes opened on her face, and Violet realized this man knew what it was to be haunted by the past. "Believe it, Violet, because it happened."

"How? Who was she? Was it…someone you loved?"

He shook his head. "I hardly knew her. We'd talked on the telephone a few times. I urged her to come to Fort Worth to turn over evidence about her uncle. We'd discovered he was trafficking a lot of drugs into the state. And we had enough to arrest him, but we weren't sure we had enough for a conviction. Lupé had the proof and she was willing to help."

"Then she came to Forth Worth?"

He nodded. "I left her in a motel room with two armed policemen. I told her I'd be back in the morning to take her to the DA's office. But morning never came for Lupé. During the night the policemen were distracted by a fracas across the street, later we learned some of the uncle's cronies staged it. Anyway, the police were away from Lupé's room for only a couple of minutes. Or so they swore. But no matter the time, it was enough for someone to silence the woman. I won't go into details of how she was killed. Let's just say I haven't been able to forget, or forgive myself.''

For long moments Violet couldn't speak. She didn't know what she could say that could possibly ease the burden he'd carried so long in his heart. And then, as she thought about all he'd been through, all those things she hadn't been able to figure these past two weeks began to fall into place. Charlie hadn't necessarily rescued her from the highway because he'd taken an instant liking to her and Sam. He was truly, as her mother had called him, the Durango Kid. He was a modern-day cowboy hero, compelled to help any damsel in distress.

''You wouldn't leave me and Sam in Ruidoso in the motel because of Lupé. Isn't that right? You imagined the same thing happening to me.''

His expression turned a bit sheepish as his big fingers smoothed gently over the back of her hand. ''Not entirely.''

''All this you've been doing for me, all this concern over Rex harming me is because of her, isn't it?''

He stared at her with disbelief. ''No!''

''Charlie,'' she said with a groan, ''be honest with me. All my life men have lied to me. Please, don't you do it, too.''

''I'm not lying to you!''

She looked away from him and out toward the barn. The gray and sorrel were moving restlessly around the dusty corral. As she watched the beautiful horses nip playfully at each other, she wished she could jump astride one of them and ride far off into the mountains. Away from Charlie and his offer of love. But she had Sam to think of. Now and always.

''Violet, I'm not confusing *concern* for *love*. Hell, I admit I've been carrying around a load of guilt. For the past few months I've been trying to save the whole world and clean it up, and in the process made a mess of myself. But not once in that time did I bring a woman home with me. Or a child. Not once did I ever turn to a woman and tell her I loved her.''

The pain in Violet's chest was like a heavy weight pushing her down, slowly stealing her breath. ''Why are you telling me all this? Better yet, why did you wait until now to tell me?''

His free hand reached up and brushed the loose hair off her forehead. ''Because tonight, when we were talking about your father-in-law and I saw fear on your face, I wanted to hunt him down and threaten him to within an inch of his life. And I knew I wasn't feeling that way because I'm a Texas Ranger or because guilt is driving me to protect you.''

Violet wasn't so sure. But it was exhilarating to think a man like Charlie could actually care about her. She'd loved Brent, and in spite of Leroy's alcoholism, she'd loved her father, too. But ultimately both men had betrayed her in the worst kind of way. Could Charlie really be any different?

It didn't matter, she told herself fiercely. She couldn't stay and love Charlie. She could only move on and hope he never discovered the sordid background she'd come from.

Desperate to get away before her tears began to fall, Violet pulled her hand from the warmth of his and shot to her feet.

''Violet! Don't you have anything to say?''

She shook her head as tears settled like a hot ball in her throat. ''No. It wouldn't make any difference.''

He snatched her hand as she started to move away, and she gazed down at him, imploring him with her eyes to understand and let it be.

"If you haven't any feelings for me, tell me now," he demanded.

She couldn't do that. She'd felt something for the man from the first moment she'd seen him cross the road to her. She just hadn't known how deeply that something was going to root itself inside her.

"Don't do this to me, Charlie," she begged.

He rose to his feet and slowly took her face between his hands. "You can't tell me. Because you love me."

If missing him while he was away, if wanting to put a smile on his face, if wanting to live the rest of her life with him meant she loved him, then she need not wonder anymore. She'd fallen in love with Charlie Pardee.

"What if I did? How would it change anything?"

"Love changes everything. It's what kept my mother and father together for more than twenty years. It's the reason they still can't bear to be away from each other for one night. That's what I want with you, Violet."

She closed her eyes, but she could not stop the tears from slipping onto her cheeks. Charlie bent his head and pressed his lips against each salty drop.

"I used to think marriage was forever, Charlie," she whispered shakily. "But I learned the hard way it isn't. Right now I'm sure you'd tell me that I'm the only woman you could ever want. But two or five or even ten years from now I might not be enough for you. I might not even be enough two months from now. So please don't ask me to try."

Before he could reply, she pressed a kiss against his cheek, then pulled away from him and hurried into the house. Charlie watched her go, and as he did it dawned on him that Angela's desertion hadn't even scratched the surface of his heart. Whereas Violet had settled in and taken total control of it.

His days with Violet were limited. He had to figure out

what it was going to take to make her see they belonged together. Otherwise, he was going to be a walking dead man.

The whole thing was a family affair, and Violet didn't belong. But Sam apparently felt right at home. He was lapping up the attention showered on him by Charlie's parents, aunts, uncles and cousins.

She'd been forewarned by Justine that the Bar M ranch, which was owned jointly by her sisters, had a big swimming pool and to bring Sam a pair of shorts so he could enjoy it. At the moment her son was paddling around like a happy duck, while Charlie's cousins, Adam and Ivy, played water games with him.

"Did you get your fill of barbecue, Violet?"

Violet looked up to see another cousin of Charlie's slipping into the lawn chair next to her. Emily, a blonde, who appeared to be somewhere in her thirties, was holding her five-month-old son. The baby was adorable, with cherub cheeks, fat legs and dark silky hair. Presently he was chewing on a plastic rattle in a way that told Violet he had sore gums.

"Oh yes. I'm completely stuffed. I've never seen so much food in my life. And Charlie said this was just a little family gathering. What does it look like around here when you have a full-blown party?"

Emily laughed. "Pretty much the same except more of everything. Your son seems to be enjoying himself. I've never seen a child his age swim so well."

Violet smiled at the compliment. "He was barely two when I started taking him to the pool. He took to the water naturally."

"I noticed he's taken to Charlie, too." She looked slyly at Violet. "Would you like to have more children someday?"

Across the wide pool Charlie sat talking with his father and two uncles, Harlan and Wyatt, and Emily's husband, Cooper. It was a fine group of men. All of them were fit and handsome and successful. Other than Charlie they were all fathers.

Violet didn't have to ask herself if she would like to be the woman to give him a child. Her deepest intuition told her Charlie was the only man she could ever give her body to. It was unimaginable to think of moving on and meeting another man who could make her forget him.

"I wanted to. But things didn't work out for me and Sam's father. He—"

"Yes, I know. Justine explained how he was killed in a plane crash."

Violet absently fingered the hem of her silk blouse. The main thing she'd noticed this evening about all of Charlie's family was how open and honest they all were. It made her feel very hypocritical.

"Well, the crash legally ended our marriage," Violet confessed to this gentle woman. "But for a long time we'd had our problems. You see, he was…fond of other women. And I was reluctant to bring another child into that sort of marriage."

Suddenly she felt Emily's hand covering hers and she glanced over at her. The look of pure sympathy on her face touched Violet more than the other woman could ever know.

"I'm so sorry, Violet. You must have felt as if you'd lost him long before he died."

She nodded, then drew in a long breath and released it. "I did feel that way. And I guess I should be ashamed of myself because I was able to get past his death but not his unfaithfulness."

Emily grimaced. "I'm sure I'd feel the same way, Violet.

If Cooper ever turned to another woman, I really doubt I could ever forgive him.''

Violet's gaze drifted back over to Charlie. Last night he'd said he loved her. He'd implied he wanted to make a home for her and Sam. But would he be faithful? He was a straight-shooting lawman, a man of morals. But if there was something lacking in Violet, if she couldn't keep him satisfied, he might change and turn away from her.

Oh, dear heaven, Violet, she scolded herself. There wasn't any use worrying over a future with Charlie. There could be no future with Charlie. Ever. She had to get that through her head.

Beside her in Emily's lap, the baby began to fuss and wave the rattle furiously in the air.

"May I hold him?" Violet asked. "It's been a long time since Sam was a baby, but maybe I can quiet him for a minute or two.''

Emily handed little Harlan over to Violet's outstretched arms. She set the chubby boy on her knees and talked to him in gentle, hushed tones. In no time at all the baby was smiling and gooing at her.

She drew him up against her chest and kissed the top of his soft head while thinking how wonderful and right it felt to have a baby in her arms. But it looked as though Sam was the only child she would ever have.

"I've got to go over to Portales this morning. It'll probably be several hours before I'm back.''

Violet turned away from the sink where she was washing the last of the breakfast dishes. Charlie was still at the table finishing his coffee. He'd gotten up early this morning and fed the horses and dog before Violet had finished cooking a platter of ham and eggs.

"Charlie, I thought you were supposed to be on vacation. That's what your family thinks, and that's what you told me. But you've hardly spent any time at home this past two weeks. What are you doing, anyway?''

He stared at his coffee cup. "I've been—seeing a few people I haven't seen in a long time. You know, old friends and acquaintances.''

"And girlfriends?'' She knew the question sounded petty, but his absence away from the cabin was getting to her, and the more she thought about it, the stranger it seemed that he was continually running off to Ruidoso, Roswell or Artesia. One day he'd even gone to Clovis, which was more than a hundred and fifty miles away. And now Portales was nearly as far. She didn't believe he'd make a drive there and back in one day just to see old friends.

He studied her flushed cheeks. "I don't have any old flames around here if that's what you're worried about. Though I don't know why you would be. You've made it pretty clear you don't want there to be…a me and you.''

She winced inwardly. With each day that passed she loved him more than she thought it possible to love anyone. Yet she couldn't tell him. If she did, it would only lead to more questions and explanations she couldn't answer without bringing the roof down on their heads. No, it was better to let him think she didn't care than to let him know she'd been living with a thief and done nothing about it, that she'd once been arrested for being a thief herself.

"I just think it odd you could find that much reminiscing to do. You must know a lot of people.''

"It's my job to know a lot of people.''

She frowned, and Charlie figured she wanted to tell him she thought his job stunk, but instead she reached for a dish towel and dried her hands.

"Well, I hope you're going to be driving into Ruidoso soon, I'd like to go with you. There are a few things I need from the store, and I want to check on my car. The mechanic should have it finished by now."

Her suggestion unnerved him, and he quickly got to his feet. "The mechanic doesn't expect you to pick up your car anytime soon. Unless something has been going on that I wasn't aware of."

She lifted her chin. There wasn't any reason for her to feel guilty about having her own car fixed. "Since you don't have a telephone out here, I asked your mother to call him for me. She said he promised to have it ready in a few days. That was last week."

Charlie practically glared at her. "I have a cellular phone here. You could have used it. Or didn't you want me knowing you were going ahead with the repairs?"

She looked at him with disbelief. "It wasn't some big, dark secret. Besides, I didn't want you thinking I was expecting you to pay me for work I hadn't yet done."

The past few days, Charlie had forgotten she was supposed to be working in order to pay the repair bill on the car. He hadn't even been giving her a job other than cooking and a little light housework. He supposed he'd unconsciously put the car out of his mind because he didn't want to think of Violet leaving. And now there was this other problem his captain had given him. It was eating away precious time with her, but there was nothing he could do about it, except solve the mystery as soon as possible.

"How do you plan to pay for it? An advance from me or Mother?"

"No! I'd never expect something like that. You and your family have already helped me far too much."

Seeing the embarrassed expression on her face, he shook his head and closed the few feet between them. "Violet, I wasn't trying to make you feel beholden," he said, his voice gruff with frustration. "I want to pay for the car. You've already done enough work around here."

She'd done little more than cleaning and plastering up a few pieces of wallpaper in the bathroom, nothing to warrant several hundred dollars, even if she included the work she'd done for Justine.

"It's not your problem, Charlie. I'm simply going to write a check. I'll have to use my bank account sooner or later. It might as well be now."

He took her chin between his thumb and finger. "What about your father-in-law and your plan to avoid him?"

She couldn't meet his gaze. "I'll deal with that if or when the time comes. Hopefully I'll be long gone before he picks up my trail."

Every word and the way she spoke them told Charlie she was frightened of the man. She'd been running when he'd picked her and Sam up on the side of the highway. She still wanted to run. If Charlie could find out what was really behind her fear, he might be able to persuade her to stay and give their love a chance. As it stood now, she was like a terrified doe trying to protect her fawn and herself from the hunter.

"You'd risk revealing your whereabouts just to get away from me," he said. "Why? You don't hate me. In fact, right at this moment I think you want me."

She wished Sam hadn't already gone outside to play with Buster. His presence would have kept Charlie a respectable distance from her. As it was, she was practically in his arms, and none of her wanted to resist.

"Is that what you want from me, Charlie? An admission that I'm attracted to you physically? You know that I am. So why do you need to hear it?"

He drew in a sharp breath as his blue eyes made a slow perusal of her face. "I need to hear more than you want me. I need to hear you say you love me."

The iron curtain she'd pulled around her heart began to melt, and she thumped her fist angrily against his chest.

"Why are you bullying me? Why can't you just leave me alone?"

She began to cry and Charlie pulled her tightly against his chest and stroked her dark hair. "Because I can't, Violet. I don't want to lose you. I never thought I would meet a woman who could make any difference to my life. I never thought I would find a woman I'd want to fight to keep. But I have."

She groaned, then tilted her head back and gazed up at the hard lines of conviction on his face. "Oh, Charlie, I can't...I do love you! I love you more than I could ever possibly tell you. But I can't stay here with you."

"We won't be staying here forever," he reasoned. "We'll be going back to Forth Worth."

She shook her head as her heart broke and fresh tears rolled unbidden down both sides of her face. "It doesn't matter where we go. My problems would follow us."

He frowned. "What problems?"

She shook her head once again. "I can't tell you. Please don't ask me to."

"But I have to ask, Violet! I can't help you if you don't confide in me."

"You can't help! The only way you can is to let me go and forget you ever knew me!"

"I'll never do that," he growled.

Violet couldn't stand any more. She pulled away from him and raced out of the house. She didn't stop until she found Sam out front, tossing a ragged rubber ball to Buster.

As she approached him, she forced her pace to slow and carefully wiped away any tears that might be left on her cheeks. Not for anything did she want to alarm her son. He'd settled in here as if it were his home, and she didn't want to upset him, even though she feared that taking Sam away from this place and Charlie was going to be devastating for him.

"Hi," she said brightly, "are you and Buster already playing fetch this morning?"

Sam grinned and nodded. "Buster never gets tired. He wants to play all the time."

I need a watchdog around the place.

Charlie's comment to his mother suddenly came back to Violet and she realized once again what a feeble excuse he'd had for bringing the dog here to the cabin. The only time Buster barked was when he was taunting Sam into playing with him.

Charlie had brought the dog here for Sam and no other reason, she concluded. Did he love her son, too?

The question brought another lump of tears to her throat, and she desperately swallowed them down and blinked the salty moisture from her eyes.

"I understand Buster doesn't get tired, but you need to let him rest now and then or he'll get too hot. squatted down on the same level as her son. "But Sam, you'll want a dog of your own when we find our new home. Remember? You said you wanted to call him Mike."

With his cheek pressed to Buster's ear, Sam said, "I remember. But we don't have to go find a home anymore. We live with Charlie now."

Chapter Nine

Charlie must have taken the cellular phone with him. Since he'd left early this morning, Violet had searched everywhere in the house for it. And the more she looked the more she wanted to scream with frustation. She needed that phone to check on her car!

The hum of a motor suddenly caught her attention and she slammed the closet door shut and hurried out to the front porch. The sight of Justine pulling to a halt in the yard was a relief. If anything the woman could call the mechanic for her.

"Good morning," Justine said brightly as she climbed the steps to the porch. "Has Charlie gone somewhere?"

Violet nodded, then motioned for Justine to take one of the rope-bottomed chairs. "I think he was going to Portales. I'm not certain. He mumbled something about it as he left. That was about an hour ago. I'm sure he'll be gone all day."

Justine appeared completely taken aback at this news. "Charlie is gone to Portales? What in the world is he doing there?"

Violet shrugged. "I don't know. He doesn't tell me what he's doing at any of the places he runs off to. Oh, he said he was seeing old friends and acquaintances. But I'm beginning to believe something else is going on with him."

Justine shook her head and from the puzzled expression on her face, it was obvious she hadn't known her son had been going anywhere for any reason. "I thought Charlie had been staying here at the cabin. Resting and vacationing. You mean this isn't the first time he's gone off somewhere?"

Violet couldn't stop a disbelieving laugh from passing her lips. "Charlie's gone nearly every day now." She looked at Justine. "Almost ever since you brought him that note. I don't want to seem nosy, Justine, but was that bad news or something?"

Justine scanned her memory, then her eyes widened as she recalled the morning she'd brought the telephone number to her son. "No. It wasn't anything bad. His captain back in Fort Worth had called. He'd given me a number for Charlie to call him back. I asked my son about it later and he'd said he'd lucked out and his captain was giving him a few more weeks vacation. After that, I dismissed the whole thing from my mind."

"Well, I can tell you, Justine, Charlie deosn't act like a man on vacation. He did the first few days we were here. But now he behaves as if…he's on a mission or something."

Justine's expression suddenly turned grim. "Damn him!" she muttered. "I wished I'd told him to go jump in the lake!"

Of all the time she'd been here, she'd never heard the older woman curse or speak badly of anyone. Something obviously had her stirred up. "Who? What are you talking about?" Violet asked.

"Charlie's captain! The man sends my son out here to

rest and recuperate and now he does this to him! I think I'm going straight home and call him myself. It probably won't do any good and Charlie would kill me if he knew, but I don't care. Enough is enough!''

''Justine, what are you talking about? Do you believe Charlie is working? Is that why he's mysteriously going off to all these other towns?''

Justine nodded as anger seethed in her green eyes. ''That's exactly what I'm thinking.''

Violet's mind began to race. ''But is that legal? Do Texas Rangers have the right or any legal jurisdiction to investigate a crime here in New Mexico?''

''If the crime seeped over the line or had originated in Texas. And obviously one has, and Charlie's captain has put him on it.'' She sighed, shook her head and tried to collect herself. ''Oh well, Charlie's a big boy. He's not like Sam anymore. I can't tell him how to live his life. It's just that I've been so worried about him and then when he came home and had you with him—''

She smiled as Violet cast her a questioning glance.

''I had hopes things were changing for my son.''

''You don't mean because of me, do you?''

Justine nodded. ''It's like Anna told you. Charlie has never brought a woman home with him. True, he does like to play the rescuer, but I got the feeling you were more. I still do.''

Groaning, Violet's gaze dropped to her lap. ''Charlie is a wonderful man. I admire his courage and intelligence and dedication to his job. I even marvel at the way he deals with Sam—and he's never even been a father before. A 'thank you' couldn't begin to repay all he's done for me and my son, but I—''

''You don't care for him in a personal way. Is that what you're trying to tell me?''

Violet was trying to think how she could answer Charlie's mother when Justine suddenly let out a disappointing laugh. It made Violet feel even worse than she already did.

"Well," Justine went on with good-natured resignation. "That's what I get for being a hopeless romantic. But I've wanted so long for Charlie to find someone for himself. Someone he can love and share his life with. And you seem perfect for him."

Violet couldn't look at the woman. "Not really. Charlie deserves someone much better than me."

"Violet!" she scolded. "That's an awful thing to say about yourself. And why would you? You're beautiful and intelligent. Warm and compassionate. I can't think of what else my son might want in a woman."

He wouldn't want someone who'd once been labeled a thief, Violet thought sadly. He wouldn't want a woman who'd discovered a crime and then deliberately run from it.

She looked at the older woman, and because she'd grown close to her, she reached over and clutched her hand out of pure need. "Justine, you're so wonderful to say these things. But you don't understand. I didn't come from a nice family like you. My father was...I guess still is an alcoholic. He hated me from the moment my mother brought me home. I was adopted, you see, and he didn't want a kid that wasn't his."

Justine laughed again but this time the sound wasn't disappointment, it was relief. "Oh Violet, how silly that you could put yourself down for something like that. You didn't have a problem, he did. And as for being adopted there's nothing wrong with that. Anna and Adam are adopted, you know. Hasn't Charlie told you their story?"

Violet was totally surprised. "No. I remember when I met Anna that evening at your house, she mentioned something about being your niece and your half sister, too. I couldn't figure out what she could possibly mean."

Justine smiled with understanding. "Well, to make a long story short, our father had an affair we didn't know about until after he passed away. Months later someone, we didn't know who at the time, left twin babies on the Bar M porch in a laundry basket. After a long investigation Roy discovered the babies belonged to Daddy and a woman originally from Houston. She was Wyatt's sister."

"The twins call Chloe and Wyatt their mother and dad," Violet said as she tried to digest Justine's story.

"That's right. Chloe and Wyatt adopted them shortly after they were married. As for their real mother, she died of an overdose of drugs in a mental hosptial."

Violet sucked in a shocked breath. "How awful!"

Her expression grim, Justine nodded. "Very awful. So you see, the Murdock sisters didn't come from a perfect family. Far from it. So quit beating yourself up."

Other than her mother, Violet couldn't remember anyone making her feel good about who she was, where she'd come from, or who she would eventually be. The fact that Justine could be so loving and encouraging, even when she believed Violet didn't want her son, was unimaginable.

Tears sprung from Violet's eyes and she squeezed Justine's hand even tighter. "Oh Justine," she said with a sniff. "I feel like an awful hypocrite."

"Violet? My dear, are you crying?" she asked worriedly. "What in the world is the matter?"

"I'm in love with your son. And he says he loves me. But I have to leave. Don't ask me why. I just do. And I need for you to help me get my car. Will you?"

Justine rose to her feet just as Sam and Buster came barreling around to the front porch. Both dog and boy were covered with dirt and Sam was holding up a rusted piece of metal.

"Look, Mommy! Me and Buster found a gun in the backyard under the tree."

Violet shot to her feet. "Where? Let me see!"

Since Justine was the closest adult to him, Sam handed her the object. She turned it over in her palm, then quickly laughed. "Well, my goodness, it's one of Charlie's old six-shooters."

She held the harmless toy up for Violet to see. "It shot caps. You know, the little red strips that pop when you fire the hammer." She handed the toy back to Sam. "Charlie played with that when he was a little boy like you," she told him.

"Oh, wow!" He thrust the pistol into the front pocket on his jeans and strutted across the porch. "Look, Buster! I'm a real cowboy now!"

Once the distraction of Sam's discovery was over Violet glanced at Justine. "What about my car? Will you take me to get it?"

Justine studied her thoughtfully for a moment. "Only if you'll promise me one thing."

"What?"

"That you won't leave until you talk with Charlie."

It was not a promise Violet necessarily wanted to keep. But under the circumstances she didn't have much choice. And in the end, she knew she couldn't simply walk away without telling Charlie goodbye.

"I promise," she murmured.

Justine nodded, then turned to Sam. "How would you like to go into town for ice cream?" she asked him.

The idea sounded pretty good to Sam until he cast Buster a regretful look. "Can he go, too?"

"Sure. He can ride in the back. But first I want you to go around to the water hose, wash your hands and face and then wash the dirt off Buster. Okay?"

"Okay!"

The boy and dog were gone like a shot and then Justine turned back to Violet.

"You realize that once we get to the ice cream shop, I'm going to want to hear the rest."

Violet nodded glumly. "I know. I'll tell you what I can."

Rex O'Dell. Violet O'Dell. Could it be? Charlie asked himself as he stared out the windshield of his pickup. The desert between Clovis and Roswell was flat, unending and presently brown from a long stretch without rain. There was nothing in the landscape to distract his spinning thoughts or blot out what he'd cottoned onto this afernoon.

Mommy says it's those damn cattle pens that do it to me.

Could Sam's innocent remark have meant Rex O'Dell's cattle pens?

Damn it all to hell! Charlie silently cursed. It couldn't be, but it had to be! There couldn't be two Rex O'Dells. The name was too unusual. And Violet had never hidden the fact that she'd been living in Amarillo.

He felt sick and cheated. But a flicker of hope in him struggled to stay alive as he reasoned that Violet might not have known about Rex. She'd implied he was not a man she wanted to be around. But had she known the Texas Rangers were after him?

A knot of fear in his stomach, he pressed down harder on the accelerator. He was already breaking the speed limit, but he didn't care. The highway was virtually empty and he had to get home. To Violet and some answers.

"Mommy, do you think I'll grow up to be as big as Charlie someday?"

From her seat on the couch, Violet put her novel to one side and looked at her son. She'd used one of his little belts to fashion him a holster for the rusty pistol he'd found beneath the cottonwood. Justine had offered to buy him a shiny new pistol in town, but Sam didn't go for the idea at all. He wanted Charlie's gun. And even though it was nearly bedtime he still hadn't taken it off.

"Maybe. If you eat the right things and take your vitamins." She patted the cushion beside her. Sam sidled up to her, and she brushed his tousled hair off his forehead. "You know," she said, "you don't have to be big in size to be important. It's what's in here that makes you a brave, strong man." She tapped him on the chest and he giggled.

"Is that what makes Charlie brave and strong? Something in here?" He patted his own chest again.

For more times than she cared to think today, tears threatened to well up in her eyes. She loved Charlie and Sam loved him, too. How was she ever going to be brave enough to take them away from here?

"Yes. Charlie has something good in there," she answered, then gave him a playful tweak on the chin. "Now, I think it's time you went to bed, young man. Buster will be wanting to play in the morning, and you'll still be asleep."

"But Charlie isn't home yet," he complained, "and I wanted to show him my six-shooter!"

"It might be very late before Charlie gets home. You can show him in the morning."

He whined a few more moments, but finally decided to give in and let his mother tuck him into bed. An hour later he was sound asleep when the headlights of Charlie's truck swept through the living room.

Violet was still on the couch, trying to calm her nerves enough to understand what she'd been reading, but she'd had little success. She knew the first thing Charlie was going to notice was her car sitting out front, and she was going to have to tell him why she'd gone after it.

While he cut the motor and walked to the house, Violet forced herself to remain in her seat and try to appear casual when he came through the door.

She must have appeared invisible because he didn't even notice her in the dimly lit room. Without a glance in the direction of the couch, he strode straight to the kitchen.

"Violet!"

His voice boomed through the little house. She jumped to her feet and hurried after him.

"I was in the living room. What's wrong?"

He whirled around, then immediately went stockstill as his eyes found her in the open doorway. For the first time since he'd met her she was wearing a dress. It was pale ice blue and cut to fit her bodice. Buttons fastened the front all the way down to her knees. Charlie's gaze lingered on the last three which had been left undone.

"Are you hungry? I fixed goulash for supper. Sam ate most of it, but there's a little left."

She started across the room to the refrigerator. As she passed him, Charlie reached out and snatched ahold of her arm. She let out a little cry of surprise as he tugged her back to him.

"What is your car doing outside?"

His voice was cold, and uneasiness swept through her like a sharp winter wind.

"Your mother took me to get it."

"I didn't ask how it got here. I asked why."

In spite of her apprehension, anger flickered in her eyes. She'd done nothing to deserve such a cool greeting. "It's my car. I didn't intend to leave it in Ruidoso forever."

"How did you pay for it?"

She tried to jerk her arm free of his grip. When he refused to let go she glared at him. "I told you I was going to write a check on my account back in Amarillo."

The grip of his fingers eased as surprise flickered over his face. "Aren't you afraid Rex will find you now?"

She was. But she was more afraid of Charlie discovering her past. "It will be a few days before the check clears the bank and the statement shows up in the O'Dell mail box. By then..." She couldn't go on. She couldn't bear to tell him she would soon be gone and out of his life.

"By then what?" he prompted. "What are you planning to do? Leave? Run from me?"

The wounded sound in his voice filled her throat with tears. She swallowed several times before she could utter a word. "Charlie, I...told you before I couldn't stay."

He lifted his hat and swiped a weary hand through his hair. "And why is that, Violet? And, please, this time give me the truth."

Her heart thumped at his softly spoken question. She knew he truly wanted to help her. But for everyone's own good she had to force herself to shut him out.

"I don't think you understand that Rex is a relentless man. He won't stop searching until he finds me."

"Why?"

Her gaze whipped up to meet his. "I've told you before! Because of Sam. With Brent dead, he wants to take over his grandson and make him into the man his son was before the plane crash. That's the last thing I want."

She seemed so innocent, so incapable of deceit. Yet during his drive home, the more Charlie had reflected on all he'd learned, the more he knew she was somehow involved with Rex. Just how deeply he didn't know. A part of him didn't want to know. But it was his job. Always his job to pull the worst kind of secrets out of people. And for the first time in his life Charlie wished he was anything but a lawman.

Clapping his hat back on his head, he said flatly, "I guess I should count myself lucky you're still here. What's keeping you now? You've got your car back."

Her gaze fell to the floor as the pain in his voice struck heavy blows to her heart.

"I promised your mother I wouldn't leave until I talked with you."

And she'd kept her promise. It didn't make sense, Charlie thought. The agony on her face convinced him she was hiding something that was torturing her. Yet she didn't love or trust him enough to confide in him.

Biting back a curse of frustration, he said, "I want to know the real reason why you can't stay…here. With me."

She groaned and shook her head. "Charlie, there are…some things about me you're better off not knowing."

His brows lifted at her frankness. "You mean like why you really left Rex O'Dell's house?"

It suddenly dawned on her that for the past few minutes he'd been playing cat and mouse with her, although she didn't understand why. If he'd uncovered something about her and Rex, why didn't he just tell her instead of trying to pull it out of her like a rotten tooth.

"All these trips you've been making," she began mindfully, "they weren't visits to old friends. Unless you use your old friends as stool pigeons. Is that the way you work, Charlie?"

He didn't answer, and her nostrils flared with disdain as she looked up at him.

"Don't bother answering," she went on. "It's obvious where your job is concerned you'd use anyone. Even me."

"What does that mean?" he countered roughly.

"We both know the answer to that. It's no wonder you haven't ever married. A woman would never know just how far down the line you placed her on the list."

Her barb fired his frayed emotions with anger and he said through gritted teeth, "You knew Rex was stealing cattle. Why didn't you tell me?"

The hard accusation in his voice crushed her far more than his revelation about Rex. "Because I was afraid to tell you."

He snorted. "Do you know how often I hear those words, Violet? I was afraid to tell. I was afraid to come forward. Afraid to do the right thing. It gets pretty old after a while."

The disgust on his face had her backing away from him, then as chilling goose bumps broke out on her skin, she wrapped her arms protectively around her waist.

"Does it not occur to you that I'm human?" she asked quietly. "That I and all those others you deal with might truly be frightened? Not everyone is as brave and strong as you, Charlie."

"Damn it, Violet, at this very minute I'm not brave at all! I'm scared to death you were somehow mixed up in a felony."

"I had nothing to do with Rex's rustling! But I'm not surprised you suspect the worst of me. There's nothing but black and white for you, guilty or innocent. No in-between."

"In law enforcement there can be no in-between, Violet. Things aren't that easy."

No in-between, her mind echoed. No reasons to justify her flight or her need to protect her son first and foremost. To a lawman like Charlie, there were no excuses to avoid your moral duty. And because he was that sort of man, she'd figured all along she could never confide in him. And she'd figured right.

Heaving out a defeated sigh, she said, "I guess now…you'll go after Rex. If you haven't already."

Charlie quickly closed the distance between them, and when he spoke again, his breath brushed past her neck.

"For your information I haven't arrested Rex. Yet. I have enough probable cause, but I want to make damn sure I have enough evidence to get him convicted."

Did Rex know the Texas Rangers were closing in on him? she wondered. If he was arrested, his chance to fight her for custody of Sam would be over. The idea should give her some measure of relief. But Rex had already warned her if he went to jail, his sister, Evelyn, would only be more than ready and waiting to step in and do it for him. Violet didn't know how far Evelyn could get with a judge. She didn't want to believe things might actually snowball to such a point. Her mind refused to imagine herself in a court of law, admitting to everyone, and especially her son, that she'd once been arrested for robbery.

"I have a feeling you could supply that evidence," he went on.

She whipped around, her face frozen with horror. "No! How could you even ask?"

He grimaced. "I was hoping I wouldn't have to ask. I was hoping you'd tell me you wanted to help me put this man behind bars."

His words slowly but surely sank through Violet's jumbled senses, and suddenly she was seeing everything through Charlie's eyes. And she knew how guilty she must appear to him. The pain of it was crushing her chest, filling her throat and eyes with searing tears.

"I wish…I know it's your job to arrest people who break the law. Especially break it to the extent Rex has. But, Charlie, don't' ask me to do this! I'm afraid of the man. Afraid I'll lose my son!"

Frustration made him give her shoulders a little shake. "I'm not a fool, Violet. If Rex is behind bars, he can't get Sam. And you could put the man there if you wanted to!"

"Maybe Rex himself couldn't get him," Violet tried to reason with him. "But his sister might. She'd certainly try. I can't take that chance."

"Bull!" he scoffed. "There's no way he or this woman could get Sam. Unless they know something about you that I don't."

The expression on her face suddenly closed, and she

quickly looked away from him. The deepest part of her was begging her to tell Charlie everything. But if he already had doubts about her involvement with Rex, what would he think if he learned she'd once been arrested for theft? It would drive the final nail in her coffin.

Defeat weighed heavy in her voice when she finally spoke, "Think what you will, Charlie. But I've told you all I can."

The need to trust her burned in him, but his training as a Ranger refused to let him be ruled by his heart. "Violet, do you expect me to love a woman who can't be completely honest with me?"

She felt chilled to the bone as the future loomed before her eyes. Charlie would be out of her life soon and there was nothing she could do about it. "I expect you to do your duty," she said flatly. "Your job. Nothing more."

Everything in Charlie willed her to look at him and tell him she loved him, that she would do anything to help him put Rex behind bars. But her head remained firmly turned in the opposite direction, her eyes frozen on the shadows in the corner of the room. How could he help her, how could he make things better when she insisted on shutting him out?

Violet finally forced herself to turn her head and meet his gaze. The anger was gone from his face. Now all she could see was great disappointment. The sight of it pierced her heart. "Why don't you go ahead and arrest me?" she asked quietly. "Your mother is a kind lady. She'd make sure Sam was taken care of."

With a weary groan he said, "Oh hell, Violet, I don't think you belong in jail! I like to think you belong here, with me. And I'm hoping by morning you'll have thought about all this and decided to do the right thing. For you and Sam. And for me."

This man had held her, stroked her hair and comforted

her. This stony-faced lawman was the same man who'd patiently taught Sam how to ride a horse, play fetch with a dog and how to simply be a little boy. But he couldn't understand her fear. He didn't love her enough to trust her.

Deciding there was nothing left to say, Violet pushed past him and hurried to the bedroom. Within a matter of minutes she had everything packed and the bags lined up neatly by the door. Then, still dressed, she lay down on top of the cover beside Sam and tried to decide what she had to do next.

Chapter Ten

The cabin was empty. Charlie didn't find breakfast waiting for him in the kitchen. There were no playful shouts and squeals from Sam or barks from Buster.

Standing barefoot and shirtless on the front porch, he stared blankly at where her car had been parked, then off to the south where the dirt road eventually met up with the highway. There was no telltale dust. No sign of anyone coming or going.

He didn't know when she'd taken her son and left. Last night hours had passed before he'd finally been able to drift off to sleep. And even then it had only been fitful dozing. He didn't know how he'd missed the sound of the car, and since it was only six-thirty, he could only surmise she'd left sometime before daylight.

Well, hell, Charlie, what did you expect? You lit into her as if she belonged on the FBI's most wanted list! Groaning out loud, he swiped a hand over his haggard face and hurried back into the house.

Everything in the kitchen was clean and in its place.

Normally at this time of the morning the room smelled of biscuits and sausage or bacon and pancakes. At the moment the scent of emptiness hung in the air.

Moving down the cabinet to the coffeemaker, he glanced over his shoulder at the farm table and immediately envisioned Sam cramming biscuits into his mouth.

Damn it, he snarled to himself, where had the woman gone? Why hadn't he anticipated her sneaking off before he could stop her? Because he'd truly hoped and believed she loved him enough to stay and work everything out with him. He had to be the biggest idiot on the whole force of Texas Rangers!

Numbly he went about measuring coffee grounds and a small measure of water into the coffeemaker. He wanted the brew strong and thick. He had to think and think fast.

He was staring groggily at the colored water streaming into the glass carafe when he heard scratching and whining at the back door. Turning, he spotted Buster's nose pressed against the screen. No doubt the dog was looking for Sam.

"Buster, you might as well quit that damn whining. Sam and Violet are gone."

The dog didn't understand or was closing his ears to what Charlie had to say. He suspected it was the latter, and he cursed as Buster rolled onto his back, stuck all four feet in the air and howled.

Charlie tromped over to the door and glared down at the dog. "You good-for-nothing, mangy mutt! I'm gonna get rid of you just as soon as I can drive you back to the ranch. Why, you don't even know how to bark. If Sam and Violet drove up this very minute, you wouldn't even know it!"

Buster instantly flipped onto his feet and let out a loud bark. Charlie cursed again. But this time he pushed open the screen and let the dog into the house.

Moments later he carried his mug of coffee into the living room. That's where he found the note. The blue envelope with his name written across the front was propped against a table lamp at the end of the couch.

Like a hungry hound snatching at a piece of corn bread, he ripped open the envelope, unfolded the single sheet from inside and began to read:

Charlie
Last night when I saw how disappointed you were in me, I slowly started to think about all you said. You were right. It would be wrong of me to let Rex go unpunished. Wrong for me and you and Sam.

I've left Sam with your mother. She's promised to take good care of him until I can get things straightened out.

Violet

Charlie read the note through three times before his mind could absorb it all. Then chilling horror began to settle in the pit of his empty stomach. Until I can get things straightened out. Dear Lord, had she gone back to Texas to confront Rex? That was the last thing he wanted her to do! The man was dangerous! If something happened to her now, he'd never forgive himself!

With an unsteady hand he jerked up the phone and punched his parents' number.

"Mom!" he practically shouted the moment Justine answered the ring. "Is Violet there?"

"No, she's already gone. Is something wrong? You sound upset."

Everything was wrong! And it was all his fault! He'd been so hurt when he'd uncovered the truth about Rex he hadn't been able to see straight. But now all the things he'd said to Violet were tumbling over and over in his mind. He hadn't behaved as a man with a woman he loves, but as a Ranger with a suspect! Now he'd put her in danger!

"I *am* upset! Is Sam there with you?"

"Yes. Violet called early this morning on your cellular phone and asked if I'd keep him for her."

Fear gripped him like a vise. "Did she tell you where she was going?"

"Not exactly. She only said she had to go back to Texas to do some things, and she thought it would be better if Sam wasn't with her. I didn't question her about it, since I figured it was something personal. And, anyway, Sam is such a joy. It's just like having you back home as a little boy again."

Charlie groaned, and the tone of Justine's voice changed to concern. "Charlie, didn't you know Violet was leaving?"

Not for anything did he want to worry his mother. At this point it wouldn't help matters at all.

"Not exactly. But I've got to find her. Don't ask me why. I'll explain everything later. Just keep Sam safe, okay?"

"That'll be a pleasure. But Charlie..." she said doubtfully.

"Mom, don't worry."

She sighed. "Okay. I won't. You're my levelheaded lawman. You always know what you're doing."

Charlie closed his eyes as regret swamped him. He'd always tried to do the right thing. But last night with Violet he'd put his strong moral values above everything. Last night he'd been too much of a lawman. Now she'd probably never be able to see him simply as a man or a husband.

"I hope so, Mom." He added a quick goodbye, then hung up the phone.

In his bedroom Charlie tugged on the first shirt he could find, then gathered up his holstered weapon. As he hurried out the door to his truck, he jammed cartridges into the pistol's chamber, all the while praying he wouldn't have to use it.

For most of the two-hundred-and-thirty-mile trip back to Amarillo, Charlie broke the speed limit. During those three or so hours of driving he'd made a few phone calls. On a notepad he'd scratched down Rex's home address, the make, model and tag numbers on his three vehicles, and the location of his packing plant. As for where he might find Violet, he didn't have a clue, other than to stake out Rex's house and hope she would appear.

By the time dusk had fallen, Charlie was eaten up with worry. For several long, hot hours, parked in an inconspicuous spot, he'd sat in his pickup, a pair of field glasses jammed to his eyes as he watched the O'Dell house.

So far only two people had come and gone: Rex and a taller, younger man, whom Charlie believed acted as his right-hand man. Though he'd never seen either one before, he recognized them from a description he'd been given yesterday by an informant in Portales.

Glancing at his watch, he softly banged the steering wheel. Rex had left the house more than an hour ago and if Violet was here, she'd come this morning before Charlie arrived. Darkness was closing in. He could watch the house a few more hours, but he was beginning to think whatever she'd come back to Amarillo for wasn't here at Rex's house. So where? The packing plant?

On his way into Amarillo Charlie had driven by Rex's feed lots and nearby packing plant. He'd not spotted Violet's car among the many vehicles parked around the place. Besides, he hadn't really figured she would want to confront the man in front of customers or employees. But she might after dark, his thoughts raced on. After it closed and everyone had gone home.

Fear crawling up his spine like an insidious spider, Charlie started the pickup and gunned it onto the main road. He could be there in five minutes! Dear God, don't let it be five minutes too late, he prayed. Don't let him lose Violet as Lupé's family had lost her!

Violet was glad she hadn't tossed away her keys to the packing plant. With them it was no problem to let herself in the front door, then on into the office, which held the company's records.

To her relief the place was totally quiet, and at this time of night Violet felt safe enough to turn on a small banker's lamp on one of the desks. She tilted the shade so it would illuminate the file cabinet, then hurriedly began her search.

She had an armload of papers when Rex's voice sounded right behind her. Fear spilled over her like a dash of ice water.

"Well, well," he drawled ominously. "My sweet little daughter-in-law has decided to come back to the fold."

Lifting her chin, Violet slowly turned to face him.

Outside, Charlie slipped soundlessly through the front door of the packing plant, then crept through the darkened rooms toward a pair of muffled voices. When he finally reached the origin of the sound behind a partially opened door, he flattened his back against the wall and carefully inched closer.

"I thought you were smarter than this, Rex," he could hear Violet saying. "These files can put you in prison. Why hadn't you gotten around to destroying them?"

Rex grunted. "You're the only one who knows about them. And I thought you were smart enough not to come back here!"

"I guess I'm not smart at all, Rex. Because I had to come back. I can't let you keep getting away with this. I want you in jail and out of Sam's and my life."

Ignoring her threat, he said, "I've had at least ten of my men out looking for you. Where's my grandson?"

Outside the door Charlie gritted his teeth. Every instinct he possessed urged him to rush through the door and whisk Violet out of there. But the dirtbag could be armed or physically threatening her. He had to creep close enough to see, then make his move.

"You'll never find out," Violet said with as much bravado as she could muster.

The man made a mocking snort, and it was all Charlie could do to keep from charging into the room and choking the life out of him.

"Oh, yes, I'll find my grandson," Rex threatened with haughty confidence. "And when I do you can kiss him goodbye."

"I'd kill you before I'd let you have him," Violet said fiercely.

Rex let out a mean chuckle. "You just might have to, honey. 'Cause when I tell the judge you were once brought up on robbery charges, he'll rule you unfit."

"I was completely cleared of those charges, and you know it!"

Outside the door Charlie closed his eyes and swallowed. So that's what Rex had been holding over her head. Dear Lord, why hadn't she told him? Because she'd been afraid of him. Coming back here and facing a dangerous felon had been easier than confiding in him, he realized sickly.

"Maybe so," Rex went on. "But the stink of suspicion will probably be enough to cause you some hell. It'll be worth a try to get my grandson."

"I wouldn't bet on it, Rex! I know a Texas Ranger, and he'll help me. With these files, he'll have plenty of evidence to put you in jail. Where you belong!"

Rex laughed loudly and Charlie decided it was time to make his move. He leaped into the room at the same moment Rex was lunging at Violet. Papers of all shapes and sizes flew in every direction as she jumped back in an effort to escape the man's clutches.

A scream ripped from her throat as Rex latched onto her shoulder. But before the other man realized anyone else was in the room, Charlie grabbed him by the back of the neck, spun him around, then floored him with a hard right to the jaw.

As Charlie rolled him facedown on the floor and held his hands at the small of his back, Rex sputtered and groaned, "Who the hell are you?"

"I'm Violet's Texas Ranger," he gritted. "And you, sir, are under arrest."

He quickly clamped a pair of cuffs around Rex's wrists, then heaved the prisoner to his feet and explained his rights.

A few steps away Violet stood trembling. Her face was chalky white, her eyes dark and wide with shock. Charlie went to her and quickly gathered her into his arms.

"Oh, Charlie, he was…" Her words trailed away as she shuddered and tried to swallow down the tears in her throat.

"It's all right, Violet," he murmured as he enveloped her in a fiercely protective embrace. "This man will never threaten you again. I'll never let anyone hurt you or Sam. Ever."

She clutched folds of his shirt and began to sob against his chest. Charlie stroked her hair and pressed kisses to her temple. Later he would beg her forgiveness. Later he would show her, tell her how very much he loved her. But right now it was enough that she was safe and in his arms. Where she was meant to be.

By the next evening Violet and Charlie were back at the cabin. The warm night breeze stirred the leaves of the old cottonwood and gently played with Violet's dark hair, while beside her on the worn bench, Charlie held her hand tightly clasped in his as she talked about her father.

"After my mother died, Daddy was all I had," she quietly explained. "I knew he was an alcoholic, but he was my father. I needed his love and did everything to try to please him. That's why I took those things to the pawnshop for him. I'd hocked things for him before, and though I knew he wanted the money for whiskey, I never dreamed he would send me down there with goods he'd stolen. You can't imagine how shocked I was when the police walked in and arrested me."

Charlie cringed at the image. The men in her life had continually betrayed her, and all she'd ever wanted was to be loved. "When you discovered Rex was stealing cattle you must have felt like everything was happening all over again."

"I was terrified and angry. And then when he started to threaten to take Sam away, I didn't know what to do. I wanted to go to the police, but I dared not. I was afraid..." Her expression was full of regret. "I guess I just wasn't brave enough to confide in you, Charlie."

He shook his head. "You're the bravest woman I know. A little foolish perhaps. But very brave. You went back to Texas and faced Rex alone. And now, thanks to all the evidence you gave the Rangers, the man will be spending several years behind bars. But when I think of how he might have hurt you...I hate myself for not handling things differently."

Violet's head swung back and forth as she looked up at his strong face. "I feel like an idiot now for not being able to tell you about everything. But you see, Charlie, the men in my family...my father, Brent and Rex, they were...well, the only thing they valued was themselves. And then I met you, with your morals and your law and will to do right.

More than anything I didn't want you to think badly of me, and I knew you would if you found out about the arrest.''

His heart full of love and compassion, he reached with his free hand to brush his fingers against her cheek. "I'm not a perfect man, Violet. I make mistakes. Lord knows I've made plenty with you. Yesterday morning when I found you gone I...you can't imagine how shattered I felt. I might be a hell of a good Ranger, but you made me see I was lacking as a man. A few kisses would've encouraged you to confide in me much better than an interrogation.''

She laughed softly because she knew without a doubt there was a heart beating beneath the badge pinned to his breast, and she knew it was beating just for her.

"Just make sure you only use that strategy on me in the future.''

His head bent to press his lips against her forehead. "Now that Rex is safely behind bars and your running days are over, you are going to be my wife, aren't you? Or can't you put up with sharing me with the Texas Rangers?''

Shifting on the bench, she brought her arms up and around his neck. "I may not share you as graciously as your mother shares your dad. But I will. I'll always be there for you in every way I can be.''

He kissed her for long moments before he lifted his head and searched her face. "While I'm away on a case, you're not going to worry that I'm with another woman?''

She nuzzled her cheek against his. "This whole thing has taught me a lot about trust, Charlie. It's a two-way street, and it doesn't always come easy.'' She smoothed her fingers over the region of his heart. "But I know what you have in here. The Durango Kid would never cheat on his girl. And neither would you.''

His expression turned purely sensual as he captured her chin beneath his thumb and forefinger and tilted her face up to his. "Now that we've got that all settled, you realize my captain has given me three more weeks vacation for breaking the rustling case. Don't you think we should use that time for a honeymoon?''

"Here at the cabin?''

Bemused at her question, he grinned. "Not the Bahamas or even South Padre Island?''

Smiling, she shook her head. "I love it right here. And then what? Will we live in Austin?''

He nodded. "Is that all right with you?''

"Anywhere will be all right with me. But I would like to come back here from time to time if we can.''

"I promise we'll come back twice a year on vacations and for every family holiday. And believe me, the Murdocks have plenty of those. But I've got to warn you right now my apartment in Austin is small. As soon as we get there, we'll have to go house hunting.''

Surprised, she leaned back to look at him. "House hunting? Charlie, your apartment will be perfectly fine for me and Sam.''

The corner of his mouth turned up in a seductive and promising grin. "It won't be nearly big enough for the family we're going to have.''

Incredible joy filled her eyes and she gave him a wide smile. "You want us to have children?''

His expression softened as his gaze searched her glowing face. "For years now, Violet, all I've been is a Texas Ranger. Being a lawman was my whole life. But I promise that's going to change. I'll still love my job and I'll still do my duty. But you and Sam, and the children I hope we'll have, will always come first. Do you believe me?''

She pressed her cheek against his. "Whether you're a Ranger or a husband you'll always be my noble Charlie. I know you'll never lie to me.''

He rubbed his cheek against hers. "Good. So how many siblings do you think Sam would like?''

She laughed as their future together danced brightly before her eyes. "What if he says six?"

Chuckling low in his throat, he began to press kisses beneath her ear and down the side of her neck. "Then we'll have to start on the first one right away."

His lips had almost found their way to hers when the headlights of a pickup swept across the front yard. Glancing quickly over his shoulder, he said, "Looks like my parents just drove up with Sam." Rising from the bench, he tugged Violet to her feet. "Let's go see our son."

Hand in hand the two of them quickly walked around to the front of the house. The moment Sam was out of the truck and on the ground, Charlie squatted on his boot heels and opened his arms. The boy ran to him, and as he flung his little arms tightly around his neck, Charlie thought how good it was to be a Texas Ranger, and how even better it was to be a daddy, a husband, a man who was loved.

* * * * *

*Romance is alive and kicking
in Ruidoso, New Mexico—
and Anna Murdock Sanders is about to discover it
for herself!*
THE COWBOY AND THE DEBUTANTE,
*Silhouette Romance #1334, is a November 1998
release—and the latest installment in
Stella Bagwell's best-loved*
TWINS ON THE DOORSTEP *series!*

Take 2 bestselling love stories FREE

Plus get a FREE surprise gift!

Special Limited-Time Offer

Mail to Silhouette Reader Service™

**3010 Walden Avenue
P.O. Box 1867
Buffalo, N.Y. 14240-1867**

YES! Please send me 2 free Silhouette Romance™ novels and my free surprise gift. Then send me 6 brand-new novels every month, which I will receive months before they appear in bookstores. Bill me at the low price of $2.90 each plus 25¢ delivery and applicable sales tax, if any.* That's the complete price, and a saving of over 10% off the cover prices—quite a bargain! I understand that accepting the books and gift places me under no obligation ever to buy any books. I can always return a shipment and cancel at any time. Even if I never buy another book from Silhouette, the 2 free books and the surprise gift are mine to keep forever.

215 SEN CH7S

Name	(PLEASE PRINT)
Address	Apt. No.
City	State	Zip

This offer is limited to one order per household and not valid to present Silhouette Romance™ subscribers. *Terms and prices are subject to change without notice. Sales tax applicable in N.Y.

USROM-98

©1990 Harlequin Enterprises Limited

HE CAN CHANGE A DIAPER IN THREE SECONDS FLAT BUT CHANGING HIS MIND ABOUT MARRIAGE MIGHT TAKE SOME DOING! HE'S ONE OF OUR

July 1998
ONE MAN'S PROMISE by Diana Whitney (SR#1307)
He promised to be the best dad possible for his daughter. Yet when successful architect Richard Matthews meets C. J. Moray, he wants to make another promise—this time to a wife.

September 1998
THE COWBOY, THE BABY AND THE BRIDE-TO-BE
by Cara Colter (SR#1319)
Trouble, thought Turner MacLeod when Shayla Morrison showed up at his ranch with his baby nephew in her arms. Could he take the chance of trusting his heart with this shy beauty?

November 1998
ARE YOU MY DADDY? by Leanna Wilson (SR#1331)
She hated cowboys, but Marty Thomas was willing to do anything to help her son get his memory back—even pretend sexy cowboy Joe Rawlins was his father. Problem was, Joe thought he might like this to be a permanent position.

Available at your favorite retail outlet, only from

Silhouette ROMANCE™

Look us up on-line at: http://www.romance.net

SRFFJ-N

**Available October 1998
from Silhouette Books...**

World's Most
Eligible Bachelors

DETECTIVE DAD
by Marie Ferrarella

The World's Most Eligible Bachelor: Undercover agent Duncan MacNeill, a wealthy heir with a taut body...and an even harder heart.

Duncan MacNeill just got the toughest assignment of his life: deliver a beautiful stranger's baby in the back seat of her car! This tight-lipped loner never intended to share his name with anyone— especially a mystery woman who claimed to have a total memory loss. But how long could he hope to resist succumbing to the lure of daddyhood— and marriage?

Each month, Silhouette Books brings you
a brand-new story about an absolutely
irresistible bachelor. Find out how the sexiest,
most sought-after men are finally caught.

Available at your favorite retail outlet.

Silhouette®

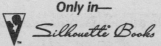

Silhouette
ROMANCE™

COMING NEXT MONTH

#1318 THE GUARDIAN'S BRIDE—Laurie Paige
Virgin Brides

She was beautiful, intelligent—and too young for him! But Colter McKinnon was committed to making sure Belle Glamorgan got properly married. Still, how was he supposed to find her an appropriate husband when all Colter really wanted was to make her *his* bride?

#1319 THE COWBOY, THE BABY AND THE BRIDE-TO-BE—Cara Colter
Fabulous Fathers

Handing over a bouncing baby boy to Turner MacLeod at his Montana ranch was just the adventure Shayla Morrison needed. But once she got a look at the sexy cowboy-turned-temporary-dad, she hoped her next adventure would be marching down the aisle with him!

#1320 WEALTH, POWER AND A PROPER WIFE
Karen Rose Smith
Do You Take This Stranger?

Being the proper wife of rich and powerful Christopher Langston was *almost* the fairy tale she had once dreamed of living. But sweet Jenny was hiding a secret from her wealthy husband—and once revealed, the truth could bring them even closer together…or tear them apart forever.

#1321 HER BEST MAN—Christine Scott
Men!

What was happening to her? One minute Alex Trent was Lindsey Richards's best friend, and the next moment he'd turned into the world's sexiest hunk! Alex now wanted to be more than friends—but could he convince Lindsey to trust the love he wanted to give.

#1322 HONEY OF A HUSBAND—Laura Anthony

Her only love was back in town, and he had Daisy Hightower trembling in her boots. For, if rugged loner Kael Carmody ever learned that her son was also his, there would be a high price to pay…maybe even the price of marriage.

#1323 TRUE LOVE RANCH—Elizabeth Harbison

The last thing Darcy Beckett wanted was to share her inherited ranch with ex-love Joe Tyler for two months. But when Joe and his young son showed up, the sparks started flying. Now Joe's son wants the two months to go on forever…and so does Joe! Can he convince Darcy they are the family she's always wanted?